Scary

J.M. DABNEY

ISBN-10:1-947184-04-0
ISBN-13:978-1-947184-04-6

DEDICATION

To those who love the Twirled Crew and keep reading.

AUTHOR'S NOTE

Although this is part of a series, Scary is a complete stand alone.
Tank is mute due to a past attack and uses ASL (American Sign Language) all his signed parts are in italic.

Happy Reading!

CONTENTS

1 ALL HAIL THE BASTARD

The music from inside Twirled World Ink vibrated the door as Gene "Scary" Sheridan pulled it open and walked inside. He shouldered off his leather jacket as he strode across the room to make his way behind the reception desk. Scary threw the jacket over the back of the chair and sat down picking up the stack of messages. He flipped through them not paying much attention. Shop manager or not, he didn't fuck with the paperwork.

When he'd hired on to the Twirled World Crew he damn sure didn't anticipate becoming the keeper of the rest of the crazies who worked there. When he heard the breakroom door creak open, he jerked his head around.

"Scary, when did you sneak in?" Trouble, artist and piercer, popped out of the door.

"Just now, glad I wasn't a fucking customer."

"The chime just went off, so relax."

That was Trouble, he was the most laid back member of the crew especially since he hooked up with his boyfriend, Brody. Trouble seemed to be on the road to permanent commitment just like the only other attached artist, Berzerker.

Scary looked up as the chime went off, he groaned as Mayor Elijah Vaughn, Brody's brother, breezed in. His perfectly tailored suit highlighted the trim lines of his body. All dark hair and clear blue eyes, wholesome and shit, *All American Apple Pie.*

"Mr. Sheridan," Elijah's smooth Southern accent and bright smile brightened the room—how fucking clichéd was that?

"Scary," he corrected a bit more briskly than he intended, but it wasn't like his nickname didn't fit him. He was a fucking beast, and he had no problem playing it up mainly to keep men like Elijah away from him. Because what he wanted to do to that slim body was probably illegal in most states, at the very least it would send the proper politician running in the opposite direction. "What can I do for you, Mr. Mayor?"

"Please, call me Elijah, we go through this every time, Mr.—Scary."

"What can I do for you?" he enunciated and knew he was a major dick, but at the moment, he didn't care. People didn't call him a bastard for nothing.

"Yes, well, I was just walking by and thought I'd say hello."

He remained silent and stared the man down. Elijah shifted nervously from one foot to the other and shoved his hands deep into the pockets of his tailored slacks. What the fuck would he do with a perfectly primped man in tailored suits? No man like that wanted to get dirty with a fucker like him.

"I better get going. I have a lunch engagement. It was nice to see you again…Scary, have a good day, Trouble."

"You too, Elijah. Hey, you need to come to dinner. Brody and I were talking it's been awhile since you've seen your niece."

"That would be wonderful. Tell Brody to call me. Keeping track of his and Mina's schedules is hard. I don't want to be—" Elijah fell into silence and stared down at the spotless, shined toes of his wingtip dress shoes.

"You're never a bother, Elijah. You can come by Twirled House anytime."

"Thank you, Trouble. Good day."

Elijah did a perfect turn on his toes and strode quickly to the exit, within seconds he was through the shop door and out of view of the large picture windows.

"Do you always have to be a dick to him?"

"What the fuck are you talking about?"

He knew what Trouble accused him of, and he didn't know why he shrugged it off as if he didn't know. Scary had his reasons, and they weren't Trouble or anyone else's business.

"You make him feel like something disgusting you stepped in. He's a good guy. A bit shy and lonely, but he's nice to me, to everyone since Brody and me got together. No better than attitude."

"I don't care what his attitude is. I got shit to do and don't you have better things to do than getting into shit that ain't your business?"

"Yeah, I do."

He barely paid attention to Trouble leaving him alone in the main room as he exited to the employee's only section.

He was a fucking asshole. They'd known it for years, so he didn't see why Trouble made a big deal out of it. He didn't have time for pretty boys in the mood to slum.

When he wanted a fuck, he found a man like him who knew the score and didn't have dreams of some fabled happily ever after in their damn eyes.

The phone rang, and he picked up the receiver. "Twirled."

"What was this I heard you were rude to a customer," his boss, Gib Phelps' voice growled in his ear.

"Trouble," Scary bellowed, and a grinning pain in the ass peeked out of the employee break room and then ducked out of sight.

"Don't yell at Trouble."

"It wasn't a fucking customer, just Elijah." Scary scrubbed his hand over his shaved head and held in a growl.

"Quit being mean to Elijah. That boy ain't done shit to you."

"He ain't a boy, he's a grown ass man who can take care of himself."

Okay, Elijah being self-sufficient pulled at the reins of possible. He guessed the man handled himself well at work, but personally he'd heard Elijah couldn't get more lost. Gib's voice jolted him out of his head, and he rolled his eyes.

"Says the bastard of Twirled."

"I'm not doing this with you, old man. Elijah's my business." Fuck, he shouldn't have said that. Scary already had too much responsibility with the Twirled Crew and his from the bar he owned. He sure has hell didn't want to add to his personal and professional workload; soothing the timid Elijah would transition into a full-time job.

"He ain't none of your business, but if you don't start being nice, I'm gonna sic Peaches on you."

Shit, to be honest, he was terrified of Peaches more than Gib. She'd worked as a public defender in Atlanta.

Her connections were a hell of a lot more dangerous than his. He joked about hiding a body or two, but Peaches knew men who could make it happen.

"Don't threaten me with your wife."

"I'll do what I want. He's related to my son-in-law."

"Trouble's not your kid, and Brody's not your son-in-law."

"I adopted all you shits the day I hired y'all. Don't make me come down there."

Scary suppressed the need to laugh at the threat. It amused the hell out of him when Gib tried to play father figure with him. He was almost a foot taller and a hundred pounds heavier than Gib.

"Like I'm scared of a geriatric canvas of skin and bones."

"Peaches, Scary's being a bastard."

He grimaced and held the phone away from his ear.

Scary huffed and tipped his head back to stare at the ceiling. He didn't want to deal with Peaches. The beautiful middle-aged woman could be worse than a mama bear when she thought one of her boys was in trouble.

"Scary, are you hurting Elijah's feelings again?"

"Dammit, he's grown and able to handle his shit. He doesn't need bodyguards."

"He's a sensitive and lonely young man. You know he comes to the damn shop just to see your ugly mug."

Scary couldn't ignore the truth of Peaches' statement. The first time he met Elijah, he would've had to be blind not to notice Elijah sneaking glances at him from under the long, thick fringe of his lashes. He'd caught Elijah moving toward him when Lucky one of the Twirled Crew tried flirting. Scary couldn't be some savior to the gorgeous man.

"I'm not ugly." He wasn't handsome either. Scary knew what he looked like; he'd stared at himself enough in his forty-three years to have every scar on his harsh face memorized.

"You're not pretty, and you're over forty, you're not getting any younger."

"I do fine." And he did, it didn't matter if he didn't remember half their names or even cared too. They got each other off and wasn't that the point of fucking?

"With your left hand probably, actual human beings not so much."

"Don't be mean," he growled.

"How does it feel?"

"Peaches, you're not going to guilt me into being nice to Elijah."

"I'm done with you, Gib, he's all yours. When he acts like this, he's yours. I'm not claiming this one."

He hung up the phone without waiting for Gib to come back on the line. He didn't have time for that shit. Scary tossed the messages back on the desk, ripped his jacket off the back of the chair, and headed for the door without a word.

He'd backed his *Harley Softail* up to the curb. Twirled World's Main Street location considered prime real estate in Powers, Georgia. For small town America, it leaned toward eclectic, and he liked it there. He'd lived there over a decade, and he hadn't had the urge to run yet.

Scary grabbed his helmet and slipped it on, he didn't have any appointments that day. A long ride would clear his head before he had to be at his bar, Brawlers, for the evening shift.

Why everyone had to jump to Elijah's defense pissed him off. It wasn't his problem the man was over-sensitive.

His unwanted attraction to the man aggravated his bastard tendencies. He'd learned decades before pretty boys were nothing but trouble. The one time he'd let a man passed his defenses, he'd been fucked over. Callum was all innocent, appeared so fucking loving, but the moment Scary turned his back, Callum fucked the first respectable man he could take home to the family.

Ugly, tattooed and scarred, Gene Sheridan was just a piece of trash from the wrong side of the tracks. Men like Elijah were all the same, and he didn't give a fuck how many people talked about how sweet and lonely the man was. It wasn't his fucking business. Scary wouldn't let a repeat of the past come around again. Elijah could stay on his side of the tracks and leave Scary to his own life.

His bike rumbled to life, and he rolled onto the deserted street toward the town limits. He was alright just like he was, and he wasn't going to change because some boy got his panties in a bunch. Clearing his head, he settled looser on the seat and lost himself in the warmth of the sun, the wind whipping around him and forgot his troubles for a few hours. On the road he felt at peace, he refused to let bullshit intrude and ruin it.

2 ALL'S FAIR IN LOVE AND SARCASM

Elijah contently smiled as his niece, Mina, raced ahead of him on Main Street. He enjoyed his quality time with her, although several weeks passed since he'd had her to himself. Since his brother Brody started dating Trouble, Mina had a full schedule. He knew he wasn't as fun as her acquisition of cooler and tattooed uncles and stepfather. Elijah wasn't jealous—much.

"Uncle Elijah, come on," Mina squealed as she headed toward Twirled.

Anytime she saw the swirling rainbow of neon as if it were a beacon, she ran toward it. But for Elijah, a wealth of embarrassment awaited him inside.

"Slow down, sweetie." Elijah groaned, he didn't want to go back in there. Scary hated him. All that light caramel, ink covered skin caused his mouth to go as dry as the Sahara. The eyebrow, septum, and Labret drove him insane. He'd never bothered to notice something like ink or piercings, but the first time Brody and his partner Trouble introduced him to Scary the man mesmerized him.

She struggled to get the door open and disappeared inside, but before it closed, he heard Mina holler. The girl only had one volume since she'd become Trouble's step-daughter.

"Daddy, Papa, Uncle Scary!" Her voice went higher when she called to Scary.

He jogged forward until he pulled open the door and saw Mina perched on Scary's arm, her arms twined around his neck.

"She saw the sign from a block away," Elijah commented.

"She loves being here, doesn't help they spoil her rotten." Brody smiled as he watched Mina and Scary. "But she picked the weirdest one to be her favorite."

Elijah caught Scary's dark scowl the big man aimed at Brody, but as fast as it was there, it disappeared when Scary turned back to Mina.

"How about some ink, Princess," Scary asked without taking his eyes from Mina.

"Please?" Mina turned the plea into several syllables, and she batted her lashes.

"In my chair." As soon as Scary set her on her feet, she was taking off toward Scary's station.

"You might as well take a seat. Scary takes Princess' ink seriously." Brody chuckled from his seat on Trouble's lap.

Elijah forced a smile. It was getting better, but he was envious of the relationship Brody and Trouble had. "Can I get close enough to watch?"

"Yeah, take my chair, it's beside Scary's." Trouble nodded toward the chair on the far side of Scary.

He'd have to pass close to Scary to get to it. Since he'd met Scary, Elijah went out of his way to avoid getting physically close to the other man. Nightly fantasies tortured him with things he couldn't have. "We have dinner reservations at the club, is it still okay if I take her? I wasn't planning to stop. I promised you two a night to yourselves."

Brody and Trouble included Mina in everything. They rarely went on grown-up dates or spent time together which confined alone time to after Mina went to bed. He thought couples spending quality time together was important. Not that he'd know; Elijah was coming up on thirty-five, and he couldn't keep a man interested passed a few dates.

"Of course. Princess isn't going to pass up a chance to see the guys."

"Princess," A growly voice boomed from the back door as several inches over six feet barreled into the room.

"Uncle Zerk!"

Seconds later loud kisses landed all over Mina's cheeks, and she giggled. For an intimidating man, Zerk could be incredibly sweet, and he seriously loved Mina. No matter how weird these guys looked or acted Elijah would freely admit they were a great influence on her.

"Hey, man, I'm working here," Scary growled and pushed the slightly smaller man away from him.

He took in the size difference between Zerk and Scary, Scary was probably three or four inches taller, but Zerk had the man in bulk. Although, the sheer size of Scary, well, scared him. He was almost seven feet of bad, growly attitude and he made no secret he didn't like Elijah at all.

Even if only to himself, he'd admit it hurt more than it should've, yet he couldn't change the way he felt.

"Come on, Eli, I'll lift you over the wall, so you don't have to pass the a-hole."

He chuckled and shook his head, Zerk wouldn't hesitate to pick him up.

"Language, Zerk," Scary warned.

"I didn't say it, Scary."

"I'll just walk around." He may be slender and a few inches shy of six feet, but he was a man, being hauled around by the tattooed brute would totally be unmanly.

"Suit yourself, your shots up to date, right?"

"Zerk, knock it off." Scary muttered without looking up from whatever he was drawing on Mina's arm.

When he got closer, he noticed the colorful lines went from her shoulder to her wrist. He knew they used washable markers and sometimes if time permitted they'd airbrush her some amazing artwork. Each guy kept a set in their stations for Mina or when they freehanded designs. He knew Scary was famous for his freehand, realistic creations. He'd seen the ones Scary drew on Mina before, and they were always beautiful. He bet the permanent ones would be breathtaking, but he'd never had an opportunity to see them.

"Do you have pictures of your work?"

Scary clenched his jaw causing the muscles to jump. "Yeah, there's an album on the counter, my name's on it," Scary answered without looking up.

He felt like the man dismissed him, and he looked down before anyone could see the hurt in his eyes. Why couldn't the man just like him? The other guys were always welcoming when he came around. Lucky even flirted with him. It was always in fun, but the man made him feel like he was one of the crew—just like the rest.

"Where's Lucky?"

Trouble answered with a husky laugh, "He took a spill on his board earlier. Priest had to take him to the ER. We doubt he broke anything, but Priest threw a fit when Lucky said he would just wrap it."

"Isn't this the fourth time in the last two months he's headed to the ER? Hasn't someone taken that skateboard yet?"

"We hid it, but somehow he always f—" Scary made a rumbling sound at Zerk, "freaking finds it."

Scary seemed to be profanity police when Mina was around. It was kind of sweet, but he knew Scary wouldn't appreciate being called sweet. Everyone laughed. Zerk sent Scary a dirty look, but the man didn't bother looking up. Scary was too busy having a quiet conversation with Mina. He'd never seen his niece sit that still—ever. Mina was in constant movement. It seemed to be another habit she'd picked up from her papa Trouble. Mina's energy exhausted him, but in the last year, it appeared to explode in an exuberance none of them contained.

It was strange how much the two of them were alike. Brody and Trouble were together less than a year. Actually, they were three months from their one year anniversary. His brother and Trouble were in no hurry to say vows but had inked wedding bands. Zerk and his partner Landon were almost two years together and, like the other couple, had gone with inked bands. It seemed to be a tradition passed down from Gib and Peaches.

Sometimes he watched the two couples and they'd stroke the simple, black inked bands lovingly staring at each other. He glanced down at his unadorned finger, and again, he felt like an asshole for being jealous. He quickly made his way to the albums and found Scary's, then he flipped open the cover.

"You okay," Brody asked.

Elijah turned to give Brody reassuring smile. "Yes, I'm fine."

"You're lying to me. You raised me, I know when you're lying to me. Like when you used to tell me you weren't hungry. Then you gave me an overloaded plate and kept a tiny portion for yourself, even when I heard your stomach growling."

"I worked at a restaurant. I had a meal provided." Elijah didn't want Brody to think about the past. They'd had what they needed, a roof over their heads and Brody always ate. He'd worked hard to make sure Brody always had what he needed. Most of the time he'd succeeded.

"Elijah, I'm not six anymore."

"I know you're not six."

"You gave up everything for me when our parents died, and I was a shit growing up. You were better at being a parent than they ever were. They were too selfish to worry about if I ate enough or if I had a normal life."

"You were an average kid, and I wanted you to stay that way."

"But how much did you miss out on? You didn't go to prom. You didn't go to college until you were in your mid-twenties. You never dated or brought anyone home."

Elijah didn't want to think about the fact he'd never dated. It wasn't as if he didn't try, but dating as a single parent sucked, especially when you're eighteen.

"I was a father, Brody, and I couldn't just bring anyone home. That wouldn't have set a good example."

"But, Elijah, you still don't date. When's the last time you just f—"

"That's none of your business."

He'd tried, so many times to find a man, but he spent his late teens and most of his twenties raising a kid. It was so darn awkward to date, and it always turned out to be a miserable experience. He had a healthy sex drive, he wanted sex, but most nights it was just him and his toys.

Elijah's face flamed at the thought. It never worked out because the man he seemed obsessed with and starred in all of his dirty fantasies couldn't stand him. How pathetic was that?

"Oh, I know that blush. Come on, we'll be back," Brody grabbed his arm and hauled him out the front door. "Now spill."

"Spill what, there's nothing to spill." Elijah suddenly found the cracks in the sidewalk highly interesting.

"Man, you do know I use to sneak into your room, and I found your stash."

"Dang it, Brody."

"So, come on, who's the hunky dude acting in those fantasies?"

"It's nobody." His face heated.

"I'm an Elijah Lie Detector, tell me, I won't stop until I get it out of you. I know your weakness." Brody cackled and held up his hands to flex his fingers.

"You wouldn't dare," he squeaked and started to back up.

"I'll have big, bad Mayor Vaughn pissing himself on the sidewalk. I'm only going to count to three and then it's on. One—" Brody stepped closer. "Two—" He took another one.

"Scary," he muttered as quietly and quickly as possible so no one would hear.

"What? I don't think I heard that right."

Brody's eyes overwhelmed his face, and Elijah wanted to sink through the sidewalk or at the very least, run away—far away.

"You heard me, but please don't say anything. I'm begging here." His eyes stung as he felt tears start to form.

"Oh, don't do that." Brody's arms wrapped tightly around him.

For a moment, Elijah sank into the comforting embrace. "Please, Brody, he hates me, and he'll think I'm pathetic."

"We'll never talk about it again. I promise, he'll never hear it from me."

"You can't tell Trouble either."

Brody pulled back with a gasp, "Oh come on, man, I tell Trouble everything. It's our rule."

"I'll move to Antarctica and never come back." He pointed at Brody with a glare.

"Isn't that a bit dramatic?"

"Maybe, but I swear I'll do it."

"You hate the cold, when it gets in the fifties you dress like you're trekking across the south fucking pole. But speaking of south poles, been thinking about Scary's a lot?"

"I hate you and failed at raising you."

"I've seen that man naked. He'd make a pain slut run in horror. Probably feels like being fisted by a giant. One ride and you're bowlegged for life." Brody's eyes turned brighter until they shimmered with tears of mirth.

Elijah gripped Brody's wrist and dragged him back into the shop, pushed him toward Trouble. Brody fell onto his partner's lap. "I wipe my hands of him. You've ruined the sweet boy I raised. Ruined him." He wagged his finger at Trouble. "No amount of soap will clean his disgusting mouth."

Brody dissolved into a fit of laughter which turned quickly to wheezing when he couldn't catch his breath. Trouble joined him.

"And I gave my blessing to this match. Where did I go wrong?" A massive arm came to rest on his shoulders.

"You didn't do anything wrong. It was all Trouble. Just remember that…it's always Trouble's fault. Besides, just look at them, they just ain't right. Princess needs normal ones like us in her life."

He turned to thank Zerk finding pink bows littered his beard and a sparkling pink hoop about the width of a pencil through his septum.

He dropped his face into his hands and shook his head. "I'm in an insane asylum." His words muffled in his palms.

"Uncle Eli, look!"

He looked up to see Mina running toward him holding her arm out. From wrist to shoulder a crimson Chinese dragon danced around her arm surrounded by lotuses and a bright blue sky with fluffy clouds. Every inch of skin covered with ink.

"That's beautiful, sweetie, Uncle Scary did a fantastic job." He resisted the urge to look toward the man in question.

"Reamed by a Titan," Brody's voice whispered in his ear before he dissolved into breathless giggles.

"Mina, let's go, say bye to Daddy and Papa."

I hate you, he mouthed behind Mina's back, and it only made the snickers louder. After Mina had made her rounds of goodbye hugs, he ushered her quickly out the door. Behind him, he heard everyone asking what was so funny, but his idiot brother only laughed louder.

"You're out of my will," he yelled as the door closed behind him.

3 THE WRATH OF SCARY

Boredom for him was worse than anything else. The afternoon lull stretched into early evening and Scary already finished all his custom sketching for the next few weeks. The welcome sound of the door chime had him jerking his head up, and he scowled as Elijah walked in with a sobbing Mina in his arms. Her face hidden against the side of Elijah's neck.

"Scary?" It was the first time Elijah used his name without being corrected. "Is Trouble or Brody around, I don't know what to do."

"No, they said they'd be taking off to some cabin overnight to get some alone time to maul each other."

He swore the man was on the verge of tears as Elijah tried to rub soothing circles on Princess' back. She wore a black t-shirt, matching tutu, striped black and hot pink tights and her little biker boots he'd bought her.

"What happened?"

"We went to dinner. I let her dress herself, she was proud and so cute. When we walked in people just stared at her and most looked disapproving. They were whispering and some bit—woman made comments about her ink and then others joined. They told me what a bad dad—" A single tear broke free to slide down Elijah's cheek as Princess started sobbing louder.

"They said I was weird and Uncle Elijah should be shamed of himself." Mina's words were muffled and broken by hiccupping sobs.

"Give her to me." He circled her tiny waist with his huge hands and pulled her from Elijah's arms, he turned her to look at him. "Hey, eyes on me." Watery blue eyes very much like Elijah's had fat tears on her lower lashes and her sadness pissed him off. Someone hurt Princess for no reason. "You're beautiful, and normal is for boring people. Do you think we're weird? Huh, are your Dads?"

"No."

"That's right. You dress however you want, and when you're old enough, and you still want me to draw on you, I'll cover you in tattoos, and you'll still be beautiful. You know what, I'm kinda hungry. Do we need a reservation for that snooty club?"

"Yes."

"Make one for ten people." Scary ordered as he pulled out his phone. He hit speed dial and waited until he heard the ringing stop and a soft grunt. "Tank, I need you and six other guys to meet me."

"Hi, Uncle Tank!" Princess got close to the phone and squealed. Tank laughed.

The Brawler Crew loved Princess as much as the Twirled one.

He gave Tank the address, and there was another grunt. "We need ties. Bring the ones from that bachelor party." A rough chuckle ended the call.

"I don't think—"

"Don't, no one hurts her feelings."

"Okay." Elijah made the call and made a reservation.

He didn't plan for them to stay long, just enough for them to make the snobs piss themselves.

"I'll follow you on my bike, the crew will be waiting at the entrance for us. You got a problem with this? Being an upstanding member of society and all that."

"No, but you know the cops aren't exactly fond of you."

"Never have been and I don't give a—"

"What about the shop?"

"I'll close down, text Zerk to come in and he'll reopen when he gets here. Let's go."

He kissed Princess' temple and handed her back to Elijah. The man and girl disappeared out the front door, he locked it behind them and exited through the back texting Zerk on his way. He didn't wait for a response and mounted his bike to catch up with Elijah.

The deep rumble of his bike didn't come close to soothing him as it normally did. Rage burned through his veins. No one hurt a member of his family especially an innocent girl for something as stupid as a tutu and marker tattoos.

Elijah was too nice for his own good, which meant Scary and his crew would need to take care of shit. He followed behind Elijah's sensible, beige sedan. It was a car that screamed responsible.

The ride didn't take long. The fancy country club was just outside the town limits. His boys were relaxing on their bikes, Tank in the lead. He'd known the man his whole life. They'd escaped the dangerous streets and neighborhoods where they grew up, but both hadn't made it out without countless scars.

The most obvious was the thick line of scar tissue that went from ear to ear, but Tank's long beard hid it. One scar bisected the left side of Tank's face. Tank got both on the same night. His friend hadn't said a word since.

Elijah pulled to the shoulder of the road just passed Tank's motorcycle. A flurry of black and hot pink flew from the back seat.

"Mina," Elijah hollered for her, but Princess was already on the move.

Princess launched herself at Tank, and the man caught her in mid-air. Tank set her astride his bike. Tank's hands quickly moved as he signed to her and she giggled. The other boys laughed at the huge, ugly biker losing his shit over Princess.

He turned to see Elijah warily watching Tank and Princess. "Elijah, this is Tank Davis, he's my head of security."

"Hi," Elijah said with a small smile.

He watched Tank do a double take and then stare openly at Elijah. Okay, that could end up being a fucking issue. He noticed the other guys laughed louder at Tank's reaction. Not many gave Tank the time of day. Tank was born ruthless, and it only grew in intensity over the years, especially after his attack. Scary knew there was more to his friend than the man let others see, yet personal shit stayed between him and Tank.

"Tank, Tank," Princess was patting Tank's massive chest, and Tank instantly gave her his undivided attention.

He grunted in answer.

"I love my tutu. Thank you."

She signed as she spoke even though she knew he could hear her. They'd explained to her Tank had an accident.

Tank signed she was welcome, and she looked beautiful; it earned the usually grumpy man a tight hug. Princess picked up the sign language quickly. He sometimes found the two of them having silent conversations when the crews got together for barbecues or whatever.

"Did you bring the ties?" he asked, and Tank reached back into his saddlebags and pulled out a mass of tangled fabric. "Who knows how to work these effing things?" He groaned as the guys chuckled at him censoring himself. Scary didn't always catch himself, but they had a kid in the crew now, so he had to at least try.

"Line up," Elijah ordered and stepped forward to take the ties, his face turned bright red as he noticed the bikini clad women.

Hell, tiny triangles of fabric barely constituted coverage, but they would prove a fucking point. Scary watched the guys line up, but Tank remained on his bike just as he did.

"I can't believe I'm doing this."

"You just might have fun, pretty man," Crave rumbled, and he noticed Elijah pursing his lips to hide what Scary thought may be an actual smile.

Each man stepped up to have the tie efficiently knotted and tightened to hang over their grungy tees. Then it came to Tank and him, Elijah's steps almost faltered as he approached Tank first.

"Turn a bit, please," Elijah's voice was soft, and he kept his head slightly down almost like he was avoiding looking at Tank.

He'd known Tank forever, knew him better than anyone, and the emotion in the other man's eyes almost looked like hurt. Tank suddenly stiffened, and Scary saw Elijah's fingertips had quickly stroked over the long, ragged scar on Tank's throat.

"You have to hold your head up."

Tank only grunted again and tipped his chin up.

"Thank you."

Tank's hands fisted on his thighs. If Scary thought he was too rough for Elijah than his fucking friend was even less suited. He wasn't going to try anything with the cute man, but seeing his friend watch Elijah with hunger in his eyes should have made him at least a bit jealous, but it wasn't there.

"Looking very distinguished, Mr. Davis."

Princess giggled and kicked her feet where she straddled Tank's big bike and leaned back against the big man's chest.

Tank's rough chuckle took him by surprise, and Elijah smiled. A sweet, innocent tilt of his plump lips.

Elijah turned to him with the last tie slung over his shoulder and approached him.

"You gonna strangle me with that tie?"

Shocked eyes flew up to his and then they rolled. "I haven't done it yet, have I?"

"Do your worst." He lifted his head as Elijah looped the polyester fabric around his neck and began twisting and sliding the end of the tie through a loop. "You're good at this."

Every so often soft fingers stroked his skin and brushed his chest through the cotton of his black t-shirt. It was not the time for a fucking hard-on. It was already a problem ninety percent of the time he was in Elijah's presence. He wanted to bend the man over every time he saw him. This was the first time Elijah was ever that close to him, he could smell the scent of soap, shampoo, but no cologne.

"I do it a lot."

Elijah sounded disgusted by the idea of wearing a tie. It was at odds with Elijah who rarely knew what casual was and Scary didn't think he'd seen the man in anything other than a suit in the whole time he'd known him.

Tank made a noise, and he looked toward his friend. The man had a silent question in his eyes. Tank was asking was Elijah Scary's boy. He wanted to shake his head, but he couldn't. Wanting Elijah wasn't new, but he sure as fuck never gave into his needs. Which for him was pretty much out of character. When he wanted something, he went for it with no regrets afterward.

"You should wear a tie more often, maybe not one like this."

"Ain't exactly my style."

"No, I don't expect it is. Come on, I'm buying."

"I don't think they'll let us through the fucking door."

"We'll see," Elijah whispered cryptically and stepped away.

"Showtime, boys. Elijah's in the lead, we'll be on his six. Anything goes down, and the cops show, whoever's closest gets Princess and Elijah out."

A round of affirmations to the plan had sounded before they were quickly on their way up the long drive to the country club's main building. They parked in the lot since no one would let some valet touch their wheels.

When they dismounted to join Elijah, he was kneeling in front of Princess straightening her tutu and uneven pigtails, even retied her boots. It all seemed second nature like he did it every day.

"Do you know I used to help your Daddy tie his shoes when I dropped him off at school?"

"You raised Daddy, he said you were the best Dad ever."

"I don't know about that, Mina. Like all parents, I made a lot of mistakes."

"Nope." She popped her lips on the p and made Elijah give a real laugh. "Daddy said you were perfect."

"The only one perfect around here is you and beautiful to top it off."

Scary watched Elijah hold Princess' cheeks and lean in to press a soft kiss on her forehead. He hadn't known Elijah raised Brody. He was aware their parents died when Brody was a kid, but he'd assumed a family member took Brody in. What else didn't he fucking know about the secretive man?

"Come on, take my hand. You okay?"

"Yeah, I got my crew," Princess stated with all seriousness.

Every one of them whooped behind her and ran up to kiss the top of her head, Princess squealed and hugged each one. They all took family and crew seriously. They'd lay their life down for anyone of them, especially partners and kids. Princess had instantly earned the rank of family, even before Brody.

They walked toward the building, all eyes were on them. Some were disgusted, and others held a hint of fear. It was the fear which caused Scary to stand taller taking full advantage of his height and massive frame.

"Mr. Mayor, what are—I'm sorry but we can't—"

"Yes, you can, I made reservations, and you will honor them. As a member, I'm allowed guests, and since these are my niece's uncles, it makes them family. Show us to a table."

"I'm going to need to talk to the man—"

"No, you don't." Elijah enunciated and squared his shoulders.

Without thought, he and Tank stepped up to flank Elijah and Princess. The host or whatever he was took a step backward. He sneered at the slim man. The snobby man turned and led them toward a long table in the middle of the room.

"No, this won't do, I need a table where my back is to the wall."

Scary knew the rest of the crew all stared at Elijah. How the fuck did he know some of them couldn't have their back to the room.? There was a loud huff, and they approached another table, that one at the back of the large dining room. All exits were in the line of sight.

Once again, he and Tank took a position on either side of Elijah, Elijah and Princess protected from both sides by them. It felt natural for them to take protective positions and it shouldn't—there was nothing natural about the new development.

"Good evening, Mayor, I'm Gloria, I'll be your server tonight, can I start you off with drinks, maybe an appetizer?"

The woman seemed friendly enough, and her smile was genuine, he could tell by the tiny crinkling at the corners of her eyes.

"Hi, Gloria, I'll have coffee, and the young lady will have a Shirley Temple in a rock glass with lots of cherries, go light on the grenadine, I'm babysitting until tomorrow."

"Got it, ease off the sugar."

"Thank you."

"And you, sir?" Gloria looked at Tank but seemed to avoid looking at his face.

Tank signed, and before anyone else could answer, Elijah spoke up. "He wants a stout."

The man seemed to instantly find the table setting interesting and started adjusting the placement of the items.

Tank once again seemed transfixed on the shy man. Scary looked away, ordered the same, and the rest of the guys ordered.

Their food quickly arrived, and they all settled into eat. Tank was cutting up the Filet Princess ordered. Scary looked around the room. It was eerily quiet, and they were the center of attention. People had their heads together, whispered and pointed, but one thing was clear, they hated the supposed unwashed masses in their pristine kingdom.

A slim shoulder leaned into him and whispered, "Please eat."

"Yeah." He dug into the huge steak and ate even though he still studied the room.

Decades of being on alert didn't end because he'd finally found a place he liked, a business and job he loved.

"Thank you."

"Uncle Elijah, can Tank and Scary spend the night at your house?"

"Wha—What," Elijah stuttered.

"You let my friends spend the night before."

"Honey, I'm sure they have to go back to work after we leave here."

"But—"

Tank grunted and cut her off, his huge, scarred hands surprising graceful as they moved—expressive. He let her know they needed to work, but she could spend the night out at the crew's house soon.

"You promise?"

Tank's only answer was resting his hand over his heart. Scary watched Elijah's expression. It was affectionate as he watched Tank and Princess. The man's behavior was confusing the fuck out of him tonight. Scary didn't like when shit didn't add up. Surprises more than likely got someone killed.

"Mina, let Tank eat his dinner."

"Mr. Vaughn, can we speak with you for a moment?"

A man with a pinched expression and a four-figure suit approached the table, two other men behind him. The hate-filled gazes traveled around the table.

"No, as you can see we're enjoying a dinner with our niece."

"We're going to have to ask—"

"Did you and your fucked up—" Scary almost laughed as Elijah and Tank reached to cover Princess' ears at the same time. "Little cult here enjoy making a five-year-old girl cry? Especially for something as insignificant as some marker on her fucking arms or an innocent outfit."

"We have a particular image, and our members are selective."

"You mean you're bigoted fucks who need a good rub-off to remove the sticks from your tight asses. Normally I like tight asses, but not when they're attached to fuckers who think they're better than Princess. No one fucks with my niece."

"If you and your party don't leave immediately we'll be forced to call the authorities."

"Go for it, won't be the first time I've spent some time in cuffs. Normally, I like my man to wear them, but whatever."

Snorts echoed around the table.

"Mayor, do you believe this is the image you want to portray, associating with criminals?"

"I was elected and served this town well for the past two years, my reputation is above reproach, and my friends aren't criminals. If you feel the need to notify the authorities over a peaceful group having dinner feel free to do so, but I assure you, you won't like the consequences. My niece needs to have dinner before we go home so I can put her to bed. Now if you'll excuse us," Elijah's voice was cold.

Scary glanced at Elijah.

There was anger burning in the man's gaze. He felt proud of Elijah and sort of weirded out by the man's defense of him and his crew. It wasn't like he'd ever been kind to Elijah. Tank still had his hands over Princess' ears as she ate dinner. Tonight wasn't the first time they'd been forced to block her from adult conversations.

"We'll be reconsidering your membership at the next meeting."

"Do what you feel is best, but after tonight, I'm sure I can find better establishments to frequent and spend my money. Now, if that is all…" Elijah effectively dismissed the not so welcoming committee.

"Very nice, pretty man."

He shot a glare at Crave. The man would fuck anything that walked, and he wasn't letting the fucker get any ideas. A dark blond brow rose, and a wide grin pulled at the corners of Crave's mouth. Shit, he was going to end up killing one of his best employees.

"Thank you, sorry your dinner was interrupted, please finish."

The rest of the meal went smoothly even though everyone seemed to find them as fascinating as a freak in a show. But they'd finished their meal, protested Elijah paying for them, although the man won with just a steely look. They filed out of the club, everyone else pulled away leaving him, Tank who cradled a sleepy Princess to his chest and Elijah behind.

"I want to thank you for what you did for Mina. It was very nice of you, Scary."

"No one fucks with Princess."

"Bad word, Uncle Scary."

"Sorry, Princess."

Elijah chuckled and drew his attention. "She has you wrapped around her tiny finger."

"I won't deny it."

"I better get her home. It's way past her bedtime."

"Yeah, we need to get to Brawlers. No one else works the front door like Tank."

Elijah turned away from him and toward Tank. Elijah approached the other man and reached out to take Princess. "Thank you, Tank, it's was nice to meet you."

His friend nodded in answer as he relinquished Princess to Elijah.

"Say bye to Uncle Scary and Uncle Tank."

"Night, love you."

"Good night you two, be safe at work tonight."

Scary observed Elijah securing Princess in her booster seat, the loose slacks pulled tight across the sexiest rounded ass he'd seen in a long time. He started to move forward until Tank's large hand spread across his chest stopping him. When Scary glanced over at Tank, he noticed the cold bastard was back. He knew the dead look in his friend's eyes hid what he felt. One thing he knew, it was almost fucking impossible to read the man unless he wanted to let it slip. The beep of Elijah's horn pulled his attention away, he watched the taillights disappear out of the lot and down the drive.

"This is fucked up."

Tank grunted, and they moved toward their bikes to make their way to Brawlers. Not only did he need to keep himself away from Elijah, now he's going to have to keep Tank fucking away as well. This so wasn't going to end well, and that was an understatement of the fucking century.

4 TALL, SCARRED AND SILENT

Brawlers was already at capacity, and it was barely eight. Tank checked the line and glared at the rowdy fuckers. He was in the mood for a fight or a fuck, mostly he wanted the second, but that wasn't going to happen.

"Tank."

Someone yelled his name, and he noticed the group making their way toward him. Brody and the rest of the Twirled Crew closed the distance.

"This is a terrible idea, I want to go home."

He perked up at the familiar voice—Elijah. He searched through the group until he spotted a surprising mass of black curls. The last time he'd seen Elijah his hair had been neatly combed and conservative. How the fuck did the man hide those curls? He instantly pictured them wrapped around his thick fingers as he fucked that slim body into his mattress.

"Shut up, you're coming out with us. We're already here, get over it." Brody smacked the back of Elijah's head.

Tank growled and reached between the bodies until he wrapped his hand around Elijah's bicep to pull him from the circle. He sent Brody a look and watched the man back up hiding behind Trouble.

"Hi, Tank." Elijah smiled shyly up at him.

He tightened his arm around Elijah's waist and then moved him slightly behind him. He signed quickly—*Touch him again and I will end you.* A slender hand patted his chest, and he rumbled.

"Ease up, Tank. They're brothers it's what they do." Trouble defended his man.

Tank just shook his head because he didn't give a shit about the excuse. No one was putting a hand on Elijah. He didn't understand his instinct. They'd only spent a few hours in each other's company, but he'd thought about the man all week. Scary warned him away, telling him Elijah wasn't for either of them. Tank didn't agree, and the fight that followed ended in a few new scars.

He communicated to Crave with a few quick hand signals. Crave smirked and winked at him shooing him away. He led Elijah inside without giving the Twirled Crew any more attention.

He sensed them right on his heels as he parted the crowd with his mass as they headed toward a private booth for the Brawler employees. He gently pushed Elijah into the horseshoe-shaped seat until the man was safely in the center with a full view of the room, a table bolted to the floor and an exit immediately to his left.

Elijah grinned, and Tank realized the man knew what he'd done. So what if he wanted the man safe, he didn't need to be made fun of for it. He frowned as soft fingertips stroked the scars and tattoos on the back of his hand. At the odd sensation of someone treating him gently, he almost jerked back, yet suspected it would hurt Elijah's feelings. He shouldn't give a fuck about the man's feelings—dammit, he was just a man, a sexy piece of ass. The thought brought on a foreign feeling of guilt.

Elijah put his fingers to his mouth and moved it away in the sign for *thank you*. Tank could only nod and resist the urge to rub his chest to rid it of a weird, uncomfortable tightness.

"Nice move, leaving us behind with your own personal Brawler Security."

Tank observed the confused look Brody sent Elijah.

"Hey, man, how you doing?" Zerk shoved his partner, Landon, into the booth and earned a backhand to the stomach.

"If I ask you nicely could you knock him out?" Landon asked.

Tank grunted a laugh at Zerk's wounded yet obviously fake expression.

"After two years of complete devotion, you're finally showing your true colors."

"Hush it, go get us drinks."

"Get Elijah the biggest drink they offer. He needs to loosen up." Lucky crowded into the booth pushing Priest in first.

Priest was looking a little sick and panicked. Tank touched his shoulder and Priest looked up at him. He signed—*you'll be okay.*

"Wha—what did he say?"

"He says you'll be fine," Elijah answered automatically. He was sitting with his elbows on the table with his chin resting in the cup of his palms. "I want coffee."

"No, you're drinking, you're going to regret tomorrow like you should have when you were too busy raising me."

Elijah didn't look like he'd hit thirty yet, so the fact he'd raised his brother confused him. He had a lot of questions and none of them he could ask. Scary was painfully clear that Tank couldn't have the man. Didn't mean he couldn't protect him while Elijah was on his turf. Pretty and innocent men didn't come to Brawlers. Cultured men like Elijah walking through the door was unheard of in the time he'd owned the place.

"But, Brody, I want coffee."

"Who goes to a bar for—"

Tank slammed his palm down on the table and shut Brody up. He knew siblings could be annoying, well, he assumed they could be, he was an only child. He turned and grabbed Zerk's beefy bicep.

"I'll get him coffee."

Tank raised his brow.

"All night, the only thing to pass his lips will be coffee."

Tank nodded and turned back to the table to find Elijah smiling sweetly at him. "Thank you, Tank."

He nodded and then tensed as he sensed Scary behind him.

"What the fuck is he doing here? Are y'all fucking insane?"

"He'll be fine. He already has his personal bodyguard," Landon answered with a wicked tilt to his lips as he looked at Elijah and him.

"Tank, I need to see you for a minute." Scary wasn't asking, and Tank growled as he followed his friend to the hallway leading to the bathrooms and office. "What the fuck are you doing, man?"

I want him—his movements were quick and angry.

"Well you can't have him, neither of us can. I doubt that boy has had anything up his ass but toys and fingers."

I do not need your permission—He clenched his fists and resisted the urge to slam one of them into the wall over Scary's shoulder.

"We're not having this conversation. It's done. Decision made." Scary spun away to leave, and Tank grabbed his arm to jerk him around. "We can't do this. Look at him and look at us, he's the fucking mayor. What the fuck would he want with either of us?"

We want him—he signed, and his shoulders dropped.

"Yeah, but would a man like Elijah even fucking think about being sandwiched by two beasts like us? We've never crossed this line."

But we could do it—Tank wasn't ready to give in—*Just think about it, okay?*

"I'll think about it, but don't get your hopes up, man. What if I say no?"

Tank glanced toward the direction they'd left Elijah with his friends. What would he do if Scary told him it wasn't possible?

Live with it I guess. Not much I can do. You are my brother, right? Cannot let a man come between that—the words killed him.

I am on him the rest of the night—he looked at Scary to see his friend agree.

To be honest, Brawlers wasn't the place for Elijah and the Twirled Crew bringing him there was a mistake. He headed back to the main room with Scary close on his heels and the proof the place wasn't for Elijah was trying to talk Elijah into coming out onto the dance floor. Elijah kept saying no, and the crew told the man to get lost—not

37

exactly working. His man met his gaze and rolled his eyes. Tank slipped between the asshole and the table, placed his hands on the man's chest, pushing him a few feet away.

"What? You claimed that pretty piece of ass? There's enough of him to share."

"Get to walking, motherfucker, you don't want to take either of us on." Scary stepped to Tank's side, he moved a step to the right. They formed a wall in front of Elijah and Tank instantly knew the fucker was going to lose teeth. He'd worked his job long enough to anticipate trouble and the drunk bastard in front of him qualified.

"He must suck a mean—"

Tank cut the statement short with one punch, and the fucker crumbled to the floor.

"Damn, is he still alive," Brody asked with maniacal laughter breaking up the question into choppy syllables.

Scary's gruff laugh came from his left, and a rough hand smacked him on the back. "If he fucking opens his mouth one more time he'll wish he wasn't," Scary answered for Tank.

A strange sense of satisfaction made him smile as he watched the guy's friends rush forward to drag him away. The three of them didn't make eye contact while they carried their friend toward the door. Tank turned to check on Elijah—*Did you get your coffee?*

"Yes, but Brody keeps trying to make me drink." The little imp had mirth in his eyes when Brody's eyes went wide with horror.

Tank turned to Brody, and the man's already pale skin turned ashen.

"I did not, he's trying to get me in trouble."

"I didn't know you wanted to switch, baby?"

"That's not what I meant, Trouble."

The Twirled Crew was fucking insane. He knew this conversation would dissolve into a clusterfuck of sexual innuendo and insults at any moment. He wasn't a prude about sex, far from it, but these guys could make a whore blush.

"Trouble bottomed once, and I think he was trying to find his happy place through the whole fucking thing."

"Lucky, motherfucker, don't you keep anything to yourself?"

"Sure, but we've heard about your unimpressive mini-peen for years, what the fuck makes you shy now?"

"My mostly virginal ass is no one's business but my man's."

"Dude, you were more concerned about them knowing about your used ass, but couldn't fucking defend the shrimp wearing a turtleneck in your pants."

Tank nearly choked, but went into bouncer mode and grabbed Trouble by the back of his shirt. Tank forced him back into his seat. Lucky hadn't even moved when the bulkier man was coming for him. He just sat there with his body appearing to lean forward casually, but Tank noticed it if no one else did. Lucky tilted slightly in front of Priest—protecting him. Priest's shoulders shook as he snorted laughter with his forehead on Lucky's back. Lucky looked proud of himself.

"Tank won't always be here, Lucky, you better learn to sleep with one eye open."

"Fuck you, man, you'd miss my asshole tendencies too much to kill me, besides you can't deny the truth."

"I'll have you know he's hung like a fucking horse."

Elijah choked on his coffee and covered his mouth.

"What kind, one of those freaky mini-horses?"

Tank looked across the expanse of the table at Elijah and nodded toward the bar. What happened next shocked the fuck right out of him.

Elijah stood on the seat, grabbed his coffee and casually walked across the table. Tank gave a small grin as he wrapped his hands around Elijah's small waist and lifted him down. The smaller man slipped his arm through Tank's, and he led them toward the bar to get out of the line of fire. He looked back once to find Scary watching them with an almost sad, contemplative look on his face. Maybe the answer wouldn't be a no after all.

5 ELIJAH HAS MADE A HORRIBLE MISTAKE

"A shot for a shot, first to puke loses." Zerk bellied up to the bar in Scary's basement. The challenge in his eyes as he glared down Lucky was amusing.

Lucky definitely couldn't take much more. The man's eyes were already glassy from the last round he'd won against Priest who was laid flat atop one of the two pool tables in Scary's Man Cave praying for the world to stop spinning. Poor man, Elijah shook his head and sipped his coffee.

"I call this one, Lucky won't make it two more shots," he spoke up and earned a dark scowl which would have intimidated him if Lucky wasn't holding one eye closed like he was picking which Elijah to glare at.

Priest pumped his fist into the air. "Ya get 'em, baby, oh fuck, we having an earthquake?" Priest groaned and reached out to grab the sides of the table. "Make it stop," Priest's squeal could shatter glass.

Elijah chuckled and earned a cute little growl/purr hybrid from Lucky.

"As the only fucking sober one around here it ain't funny making fun of the lightweights," Scary whispered in his ear.

He almost jumped out of his skin but caught himself before he flinched. He found himself trapped between two massive bodies. His shoulders tightly pressed to Scary and Tank's biceps. He found himself too aware of his lack of height and bulk, yet he didn't feel uncomfortable or afraid. In the past week, the casual acquaintance shifted between him and the two men, maybe not friendship but something close.

"I'm not making fun, and Lucky's a lightweight. I'm surprised he's making it to the next bracket."

Loud, piteous moans came from the pool table.

"Priest, if I have to replace the felt again I'm going to take the cost out of your ass."

"That's my ass," Lucky growled.

He wasn't the only one giving Lucky a strange look. Well, that's interesting, he thought and then Lucky and Zerk started throwing the shots back Trouble was pouring. One, two—it happened in slow motion, Lucky steadily tipped back as if the weight of his head dragged him backward.

"Man down!" He laughed and held out his hand, and Landon placed a twenty on his palm.

"You bet against me," Zerk's offended tone drew an unapologetic and strangely innocent look from Landon.

"But, baby, with Lucky's background, I thought it was a sucker bet on Elijah's part."

"You placed a bet against Lucky," Scary asked.

"Yeah, Zerk has him by about a hundred pounds or more. Also, Lucky almost took a header off his stool before Zerk stepped up."

"What are you going to do with your ill-gotten gains?"

"Don't know, Mina—"

"Princess," everyone corrected.

"Yes, Princess wants a new helmet like yours and Tank's, so I thought I'd put it toward that. But of course, she wants her half-helmet with a base of hot pink under the skulls. You did the work, right?"

"Nope, that'd be Tank."

He turned to find Tank watching him, and he didn't recognize the look in the man's dark, forest green with their flecks of yellow eyes. Tank's face impassive and he caught himself before he reached to stroke his fingertips along the ragged scar. He was losing his mind. Was it just a week ago he'd fostered an idiotic crush on Scary? He couldn't develop one on Tank too. Elijah probably already reached the point of no return in the crush on Tank department. Elijah was going to die a virgin, and at the thought, he dropped his chin to hide his frown.

Thick fingers with rough callouses slipped beneath his chin and tilted his head back up to meet Tank's gaze. His coffee mug disappeared.

Tank removed his fingers and signed—*ask me?*

"Would you do—"

"You're with me." Brody swooped in and dragged Elijah from his perch between the two men he couldn't want.

Two hands gripped his hips, one was Scary's and the other belonged to Tank. Two terrifying growls rumbled behind him before Brody pulled him farther away. He nearly tripped on the steps as his brother roughly hauled him upstairs and then quickly through the house to exit the back door.

"What the fuck is going on?" Brody barked out the question.

"I don't know what you're talking about. I was getting ready to ask Tank to paint a new helmet for Mina. She wants one like theirs."

"That's not what I'm talking about."

"Then tell me because I'm clueless here."

"Tank, and disturbingly enough, Scary."

He roughly pushed his hands through his hair and tugged the curls a bit. He was confused.

"Elijah, Scary brought the Brawler Crew to the rescue two weeks ago. Last weekend Head of Brawler Security is your personal bodyguard, and now you're all cozy between Scary and Tank. I know you've been thinking about being pounded by the inked bad boy, but are you going bigger and get reamed by a second dick?"

"Brody." He didn't bother hiding his hurt.

"Don't Brody—"

"Brody," Trouble's pissed off voice came from the opened back door.

He'd never heard Trouble angry before especially not with Brody. Luckily it appeared no one else was with him. He would have died completely of embarrassment or made his Antarctica plans if Brody humiliated him in front of the group of people he wanted to consider friends.

"Trouble, he's losing—"

"Your brother's a grown ass man, and what he does or who he does it with isn't anyone's business but him and his partner or partners."

Elijah's face caught fire at the mention of partners. Did everyone think he wanted both men? Did Brody let Elijah's secret slip in front of Trouble?

"There's no partners," he squeaked.

"Elijah, go back inside. Everyone's getting ready to pile up and watch the gory-fest. Tell them not to wait. I need to talk to Brody."

"Elijah," Brody called his name, but he didn't turn around to face his brother.

"I just wanted one night without expectations, of living by someone else's rules. Tank is a very nice guy. Scary and the Brawler Crew went above and beyond for Mina, and me too. I know I'm not like you and the guys, but I almost felt like a fit, even if it was for only a few minutes. Sorry I messed up and turned into a sudden disappointment."

He didn't wait for an answer and rushed back into the house, he wiped away the hurt he felt and plastered on that fake politician smile he'd become adept at over the last few years. He remembered his first night at Brawlers, and the way Tank hadn't treated him like the Mayor and Elijah didn't have to pretend to be something he wasn't. Even Scary came to his defense, he'd finally felt like a part of the group he'd been jealous his brother belonged to since Elijah had met them. He had no delusions he would start anything with either Scary or Tank, but dammit even for five minutes, he wanted to be one of the crew. It wasn't in the cards, and he should've remembered it.

♦ ♦ ♦

Summers in Powers, Georgia were always miserable, it was only the tail end of Spring, and the temperatures were soaring, but the humidity was killer. Elijah couldn't sleep because, essentially, he was in a cuddle pile surrounded by huge bodies putting out way too much body heat. He wanted his fan and his AC at 68. Landon turned over about twenty minutes ago, and Zerk quickly followed, the heavy, hot arm rested over Landon and him. Who would have thought these frightening looking men would be snugglers?

He was going to have a heatstroke before morning and his day was going to suck. None of the guys had to be at work before noon or had to go in at all. His head was too full of Brody's accusation.

During the movie, he'd set on the floor in front of one side of Scary's enormous sectional. Scary and Tank once again plopped down on either side of him, their knees leaned against his shoulders. He'd swore at one point fingers played with his hair, but when he turned around, they were both focused on the carnage on screen.

Maybe he shouldn't have had those last five cups of coffee. He wiggled his way out from under Zerk's arm and away from Landon's hands fisted in the back of his t-shirt. Turning his head, he found himself inches from Tank's face, and if he leaned slightly, his lips would almost touch the other man's. He scrambled quickly to his feet and went in search of the bathroom.

He was losing whatever he had left of his mind. A year earlier, Elijah had everything right on schedule, his life perfectly planned, but one inappropriate crush and now a second. He lost his balance.

Scary's house wasn't large. It was a newer remodeled house in an older neighborhood. Very bachelor chic, but Scary was surprisingly tidy—nothing out of place. He softly walked toward the hallway. A sliver of dim light shined through the tiny crack in a door at the end of the hall. He pushed it open slowly and froze in mortification at the sight of Scary naked, his covers pushed to the foot of the bed.

He could deal with a naked Scary, but the hand around a thick—Elijah tried to back away only to collide with someone. He didn't know why, but he knew it was Tank. An arm moved around his waist, and a hand, the size of a baseball mitt, splayed open on his stomach. His head perfectly tucked beneath the big man's chin. His dick jumped at the closeness of Tank's frame and the hard length pressing into his lower back.

His body started to shake. He didn't know if it was shock or whatever but he couldn't take his gaze away from the scene playing out before him. Scary loudly groaned from the bed and seemed to echo in the eerie quiet of the house. Scary pressed his feet flat on the bed as he pushed and pulled his pierced cock through his fist. He tried to look around, but Tank's hand took hold of his jaw and forced him to keep watching.

"Please don't," the pleading in his whispered words ignored by Tank.

Tank's hand stroked down until the man's pinkie stroked the head of his cock and his hips jerked. He must have made a sound loud enough to draw Scary's attention because dark, glittering eyes pinned him. Instead of what he thought would happen—Scary yelling at him and flying from the bed, he continued to stroke his cock—faster and harder. Elijah's breathing turned ragged.

He pushed back, trying to escape, but hips flexed, and Tank's cock rubbed against his back. Tank's lips and teeth teased his ear. Elijah felt like his body was going to shake apart. Heat infused him, and sweat dampened his forehead, started to make his clothes feel uncomfortable. The whole while Scary watched him. Scary and Tank stayed silent except for groans and animalistic rumbles.

Tank's hand dipped beneath the waistband of Elijah's pajamas, and as the man completely cupped his dick, he nearly lost it, especially when Scary shouted Elijah's name and white splattered the hair on Scary's cut six-pack. Tank started to walk him into the bedroom and Elijah couldn't breathe.

An overwhelming sense of humiliation caused him to fight, and he spun out of Tank's embrace. Whatever happened next was a blur. Somehow, he'd gathered his overnight bag, keys and phone. He found himself in his car speeding across town in the middle of the night. His heart pounded, and his cock throbbed, his hands shook and tightened around the steering wheel.

Burning embarrassment mixed with a desire to the degree he'd never felt before. They couldn't want him, it was all a huge joke. But he couldn't forget the fleeting moment he'd wanted to give in as Tank took him into Scary's room.

Tears slipped from the corners of his eyes as he realized Brody was right, Elijah wanted both men and how pathetic did that make him?

6 THEIR BOY WAS ON THE RUN

He and Tank sat on one of the couches in Twirled and propped their booted feet on the table. A few days ago, things went a little off track. Okay, they'd veered into an oncoming semi. He hadn't agreed aloud to Tank's claim Elijah was theirs, but he couldn't deny it. He'd fought his attraction for months and fuck, he grew tired of fighting.

Being a sharer wasn't really in his damn nature. He and Tank had gone after the same piece of ass in the past, but never with the intention of keeping him or sharing.

Tank grunted to get his attention, and he looked toward him.

We fucked up.

"That's the fucking truth." It wasn't the first time he'd jacked off to thoughts of Eli. Getting off for him was about releasing some tension. It wasn't about picturing some cute man's ass spread wide by his cock. "So, we getting our fucking boy or give up on this fucked up plan of ours?"

Do we have a plan—Tank signed.

Scary shook his head and turned away. Did the poor guy even know what they were thinking or was what happened just a fuck up? He knew Elijah wasn't planning to catch him. Scary had let down his guard and surrendered to his favorite vision of Elijah bent over his desk, then Elijah was there for real. Tank behind Elijah and the two of them were sexy as fuck together. Elijah's lips had parted as Tank grabbed his dick and the innocently sexy flush on the beautiful man's cheeks set him off embarrassingly quick.

Trouble breezed through the door.

"Scary, Tank," he greeted them, but didn't look at them. He stopped in his tracks and turned toward them. "Okay, what the hell is going on?"

"What do you mean?"

"Don't play stupid because I sure as fuck know neither of you are."

"He's our boy. That's all you fucking need to know."

"I need to know more than that. He's my brother-in-law. Brody ain't happy with Elijah, and they had a few words."

"What did Brody do to Eli," his voice was deadly calm when he asked.

"Don't use that threatening tone with me. We all know Eli's had a bit of a crush on you for a while. Even though you tried to ignore it, it was kinda obvious, but this new thing with Tank, well, we're worried about him. We don't think Eli has any—"

"We know our boy—" Scary glanced at Tank to find the man smirking. "Is untouched."

"Okay, Tank, knock it off. That's a bit creepy." Trouble placed his hands on his hips.

Tank shrugged his massive shoulders and chuckled.

"We need his number."

"I don't know about that. Maybe you should ask him yourself."

"His number now. Can't take our boy on a date without asking him."

Dating was a new experience for them, his one serious thing he'd had with Callum didn't qualify as dating. Elijah required dates and probably romance. What the fuck did they get themselves into?

"This ain't about y'all just having some fun with Eli, right? He's terminally shy and getting his ass-cherry popped is sorta a big thing especially is it's the two—" Trouble shuddered. "Okay, that's just fucked up, and I never want to think about it again."

"You think about our dicks often, Trouble?"

"Don't make me puke, man."

He laughed as the man did turn a bit green. Trouble held out his hands for their phones, Tank and him handed them over for Trouble to program in Elijah's number.

"If anyone asks, you stole it from my phone."

"Deal." They took their phones back.

"Also, text him because he never answers his phone unless it's work related."

"We got this, get to work. You got a one o'clock."

Trouble shuffled off to the back room. Scary turned to Tank to find the man watching him.

"Are we doing this damn thing? Because I gotta be honest, I'm wondering if we're gonna be fucking up our boy's life."

They were both hitting their early forties that year. They didn't exactly have the most respectable fucking jobs. Elijah was an upstanding member of society. The damn mayor at that. How the fuck would Elijah handle two partners with sketchy criminal backgrounds and who ran a bar the cops staked out every weekend? They didn't even know if Elijah was out of the closet and they'd been out of the closet for over twenty years. It was one of the reasons scars marred Tank's face and body.

Tank showed him his phone and the text he sent. His friend wasn't wasting any time.

Tank: *Elijah, let's talk*

Scary typed out his message for Elijah. *Meet at Brawlers tonight—Scary*

The rest of the guys filed in along with Landon and Brody, Princess ran over and plopped down between him and Tank.

"What happened to your hair," Scary asked and scowled at Lucky. She had beads, colorful thread wraps and braids mingled through her long curls.

"I let Lucky take her to the park yesterday," Brody grumbled.

"I love it, it's so pretty," she squealed and touched her hair. "Papa's piercing my ears today. I picked out rainbow hoops."

"She's fitting in a little too well around here," Brody said as he walked off.

"Hey," they all said in unison and Brody threw his hands in the air.

"I had a positively sweet five-year-old, less than a year later, I have a sidecar riding, tattoo loving hippie in training."

"You make it sound like that's a bad thing." Lucky pouted.

"I want to show Uncle Elijah when my ears are pierced."

"I'll send him a picture," Scary assured her.

She hopped off the couch after giving him and Tank tight hugs then went to take a seat in Trouble's chair. Lucky came up behind her to gather her hair up and twisted it atop her head like he normally wore it.

"I hear our beautiful granddaughter is getting her first piercings today." Peaches' voice echoed sweetly around the shop as her and Gib's came in the back door. "Oh my, look how beautiful she is." Peaches pushed through them and touched Princess' hair. "Nice job, Lucky."

"Thank you, at least someone appreciates my efforts."

"Okay, make room so we can get those ears pierced." Trouble walked up with gloves, sterilized metallic rainbow hoops, and a sealed needle.

Scary took the hand she held out. Today wasn't the first time she'd been around someone getting pierced and knew what was going to happen, but her tiny hand shook in his.

"Hey, Princess. You look at me and nowhere else, okay?"

"She's my daughter, Scary."

He turned his head to whisper in Brody's ear. "Drop the attitude. We're not exactly on friendly terms right now."

The man knew what was good for him and shut his mouth. Trouble was a master at his job, and before Princess could even flinch, he had both hoops in and secured. There were a few tears on her lashes. He kissed the back of her hand. "Wipe those little tears away, and we'll take a picture for Elijah."

She swiped at her cheeks and then put on a big smile, he took a quick picture and sent it to Eli. He straightened and stepped back to let everyone make a fuss over her. It wasn't long before he received a response, his phone chimed, and Tank was right beside him.

Elijah: *She's beautiful! Tell her, please. Love her hair. Wished I was there.*

Another text followed. Elijah: *What time?*

Scary: *Nine.*

Elijah: *Okay. Have to get back to work.*

"You better hope this works, man."

Tank slapped him on the back and headed for the door. He waved over his shoulder as everyone told him bye. Scary went to work and hoped like fuck the day went quickly.

◆ ◆ ◆

Tension built among the crowd. The room packed as it always was. Brawlers boomed in the small town when he and Tank bought the old owner out. Tank had worked as a bouncer since they'd settled in Powers a decade before. The place was on the rough side, but it always had been, and they were equipped to handle it. Fighting is what Scary and Tank knew best. He sipped his beer and kept his eye on the entrance.

They still had a few minutes before nine, part of him doubted Elijah would show up. Although Scary doubted Elijah ever went back on his word after he made a promise.

His phone beeped, and he pulled it from his back pocket to read this message.

Tank: *He's here. We're coming in.*

Ordering a cup of coffee and another beer for him and one for Tank, he grabbed them. He went to stand by their booth, he tracked Tank's movements, and when he broke through the mass of bodies, Elijah was tucked beneath his arm. Elijah looked nervous as hell as he wrung his hands in front of him.

"Elijah," Scary greeted him, but Elijah wouldn't look at him. He curled his fingers and pushed them beneath Elijah's chin to lift the man's gaze to his. "None of that shit, Elijah." He looked down at Elijah's full lips and leaned down to brush a kiss to the full curves. "Have a seat," he whispered, and then he steered Elijah into the booth. Tank and he slid in on either side of the horseshoe seat. "Coffee." He nudged the mug toward Elijah.

"Th—thank you, I'm—I'm sorry about—"

Scary watched Tank stroke the backs of his fingers down Elijah's cheek.

"Don't fucking apologize. It's best you ran. If we'd gotten you in my room, we wouldn't have let you leave before we found out what that tight ass felt like around our cocks."

Elijah choked, and Tank sent him a dirty look. He wasn't the subtle fucking type, but neither was Tank. "He'll have to get used to it sooner or later."

"What is going on here?" Elijah sounded so small and frightened.

"We're dating."

Scary didn't ask because Elijah wouldn't admit it, but he knew damn well Elijah belonged to them.

"Dating," Elijah's voice cracked. "Who am I dating?"

"Us. We want you, and we're willing to share because neither of us is going to let the other have you alone."

"Share? What is this porn?"

Tank laughed at the question, then tapped Elijah on the shoulder. He began to sign—*Talking is not Scary strong suit. We want you. We are friends. I would hate for Scary to have you when I want you too. We share.*

"I—I don't know if I can do that."

"Why not," Scary asked.

"I'm not like that."

"Like what? I know we ain't any fucking prize. We're both a bit on the ugly side especially Tank."

"There's nothing wrong with Tank."

Scary suppressed his grin at the anger making Elijah's eyes shine. "So, I'm the ugly one huh?"

"That's not what I said."

"So, Tank really is the hideous one."

Slender hands shoved against his chest, and Elijah leaned back into Tank. Scary felt a hand brush his leg and he looked down to find Tank spreading his hand on Elijah's hip. He waited to feel anger or jealousy, but neither emotion made an appearance. Doubts still lingered for Scary about the whole threesome relationship working, but some of it was put to rest. "You can't lie and say you don't fucking feel something for both of us."

"No, I can't say that, but all this is—" Elijah motioned to the three of them, "it's weird."

"It's only weird if we think so. Tank and me are on board for whatever, but we also don't know if you're out of the closet. You're mayor, and we're not exactly the partners for someone like you."

"Brody said I was crazy." Elijah's fingers twisted at the hem of Scary's t-shirt and tugged slightly.

"For what?"

"I told him I had a crush on you about a month ago and then he saw...noticed the way I looked at Tank or something. He made some—" Elijah paused, and his face turned bright red.

"What did he say," Scary growled the question and met Tank's gaze. There was anger on Elijah's behalf there too.

"He made sexual comments about me being reamed. This is embarrassing."

"Nothing to be embarrassed about. What happens in bed between us is our business, definitely not Brody's."

"Who says anything's going to happen?"

"We do."

Tank grunted his agreement.

"And if I say no."

"Not going to happen."

"For someone that doesn't like me, you're pretty quick to want to get into bed with me."

"I've wanted you in my bed since the minute you walked into Twirled. I almost mussed that perfectly pressed suit of yours." He leaned in and scraped his scruff over Elijah's smooth cheek. "Just imagine your pale ass with my hand print on it, stretched wide by my cock. I bet you'd beg me for more, scream for Tank to give you more. So, say yes, because that hard-on you're rocking tell me you want to."

Elijah moaned, and Scary retreated enough to see his face, the small man tilted his head, and Scary noticed Tank nuzzling the side of Elijah's throat.

"I—I require dates."

"Whatever you want, we'll pick you up Sunday. You're going riding with us."

"Really?"

The longing in Elijah's voice made his chest tighten.

"Yeah, you'll ride with one of us on the first half and the other on the way back. Your choice."

"What if I choose wrong?"

"No wrong choice." Scary straightened and placed his hand on Elijah's slim thigh, stroking upward until he pressed to the side to Elijah's cock. His boy's hips jerked. "Easy, you sure you require dates?"

"Yes." The nervousness made Scary back off. A man like Elijah needed a softer touch—romance. It wasn't their strong suit, but for Elijah, they'd try. It didn't mean they couldn't have some fun with their boy in the meantime.

7 ELIJAH'S FIRST RUN

The sun warmed Tank's face as he tipped his chin upward and took a deep breath. He was nervous as fuck about a date with Elijah. It wasn't like he knew anything about dating. Before the one-night-stands grew tiresome, he'd taken home a few guys from Brawlers, but fucking wasn't dating.

Dating required conversations, mutual interests and attraction. For obvious reasons communication wasn't his strong suit. American Sign Language wasn't required unless someone knows or works with people who are hearing impaired. He'd given up years ago on finding a partner. Having something more than meaningless sex seemed impossible.

He shifted on his bike and rubbed his palms up and down his thick thighs. Everyone was showing up to Scary's house, then they'd head out. The destination was unknown. Since they'd started the tradition three years ago when they solidified the permanent Crew of Twirled,

Sundays they'd head out with no plan. The other guys insisted he come along. Although Tank didn't come out every week, he tried to join them at least once a month.

Today was different though. Elijah was coming along for the first time. Elijah seemed like a part of the tight-knit group but kept himself apart from it too. He wondered why the good-looking man appeared so shy when he should be on top of the world. There were always what-ifs and whys, but often there weren't any clear answers.

He turned to look over his shoulder as he heard a car approach. Tank stood, swung his leg over his bike, straightened and made his way toward Elijah's vehicle. Scary joined him and opened the driver's door.

Elijah wore a pair of surprisingly worn pair of jeans and a faded navy t-shirt that formed to a slender frame. He even wore a pair of boots.

"Hi, sorry I was a few minutes late." Elijah apologized as he slid from the seat and straightened.

Scary stepped closer to Elijah, he lifted his hand to tip Elijah's head back and leaned down. They looked good together. Scary's rough, hardness contrasted perfectly with Elijah's softness. When their mouths touched, Tank waited for any jealousy, yet it wasn't there. Scary's hand stroked across Elijah's cheek and curved around the smaller man's nape. The kiss deepened, and Scary pressed Elijah back against the car. Elijah's sexy moan drew Tank closer and then the kiss ended. Scary moved away slowly, and Tank took his place.

"No problem. Lucky's lazy ass is about to get kicked to wake him up."

Elijah stared at Scary and him with his kiss darkened lips swollen. "Am I dressed okay, I had to borrow some things from Brody."

You look perfect—Tank signed.

"Thank you."

He lifted his left hand to gently stroke his index finger along Elijah's smooth jaw. Tank slowly lower his mouth to Elijah's giving his man plenty of opportunity to say no. Part of him waited for the rejection. Elijah knew Scary longer. The attraction there for months before he'd ever earned Elijah's attention.

Elijah's soft, hesitant fingertips caressed over his beard, and he closed the distance. Fuck, he'd never found anything half as sweet and perfect. His cock instantly hardened, and he pushed his tongue against the seam of Elijah's lips. Slender hands clutched at the back of his neck. He lowered his hands to Elijah's waist, lifted him and took a few steps to the left to set Elijah on the hood.

Slim thighs gripped his and Tank pushed his aching dick to Elijah's flat stomach.

"Fake Tattooed Jesus, can't anyone keep it in their pants?" Lucky snorted behind them.

Elijah started to pull away, but he wasn't having any of that bullshit. The kiss spiraled out of control and Tank couldn't care less. He leisurely eased the heat until he backed away laying his forehead against Elijah's and tried to catch his breath. Flexing his hips, he showed Elijah exactly what he did to him. He was about to say fuck the ride and drag his man into the house.

He lifted his hand to cup Elijah's cheek and dragged his calloused thumb across the plump lower lip.

"Fuck the ride. Let's take our boy inside."

Tank shook his head. *We promised our boy a ride*—Tank signed to Scary but kept his eyes on Elijah. A small smile curved the man's beautiful lips.

"Fine, but afterward all bets are fucking off."

Tank nodded.

"You get him the first half. Let's gather these lazy fucks up." Scary leaned forward and pressed a rough kiss to Elijah's mouth. He turned away and hollered at everyone to get their butts moving. The whole crew chuckled at Scary censoring himself as Mina ran out of the house with her tiny hot pink and Skull helmet dangling from her hand. She looked like a mini-bad ass biker.

"Elijah…" Brody's voice caused Tank to spin. Trouble's arm slung across the cute man's shoulders.

The fact Elijah raised Brody still piqued his curiosity. One day he hoped to get the story, but the three of them hadn't spent much alone time together yet.

"Brody, thanks for dropping the clothes by the house."

"I'm just glad they fit. You've got a few inches in height on me."

"You always got your pants too long."

"I wished for a few more inches in height. Hey, Tank." Brody nervously glanced at him.

Tank was confused. They'd always been on friendly terms since he'd met Brody almost a year ago. He'd come to think of them as friends. Maybe Brody wasn't happy he and Scary were involved with Brody. He knew it wasn't normal, but Tank wanted whatever happened between them and Elijah to work.

"Uncle Elijah, Uncle Tank." Mina sailed through the air and Tank barely caught her, then spun her around.

He settled her on Elijah's lap.

Princess, love your new leathers—Tank signed and then tickled her sides as Elijah held her tight to his chest.

"Thanks, are you Uncle Elijah's boyfriend?"

Yes—He didn't even hesitate when he answered. It felt a bit weird. He'd never had one before.

"But isn't Scary his boyfriend too?"

He glanced at Elijah, Scary, and then back to Brody and Trouble.

"This one is all on y'all, man." Trouble held up his hands and steered Brody across the yard.

We both like your Uncle Elijah—He didn't know how to explain, but also didn't want to lie to their Princess.

"We want to spend time with Elijah."

Mina scrunched up her forehead and tilted her head to the side. "Would you still be my uncles?"

"Always. Nothing changes. I like Uncle Tank and Scary like your Daddy likes Papa."

"Daddy loves Papa, okay, but you can't fight and go away okay?"

"Promise," Elijah pressed his lips to the top of Princess' head.

Tank watched Elijah and Princess together. Family wasn't a concept he'd understood before becoming friends with the Brawler and Twirled Crews.

"Time to get your helmet on, Princess. We have a long ride before lunch."

"Okay, Uncle Scary."

Princess wiggled to get off Elijah's lap, and Tank picked her up to set her on the ground. She took off running as she pulled the hemp tie from her hair letting her hair down. He shook his head as the heavy mass of braids, thread wraps and beads shone under the morning sun before she covered it up with her helmet.

"She's so much like Brody at that age."

"We know your parents died, wasn't there anyone else to take Brody?"

"No, our parents were only children." Elijah paused. "They weren't the responsible type—spoiled. I don't even know why they named me as Guardian in their wills."

"So, you took over."

"I'd already taken over. Brody was mine from the time our parents brought him home. I was twelve and responsible for him while they continued with their trips and parties. By the end, they'd already blown through most of their inheritance and trust funds, and also the college fund our grandparents set up. What little was left over paid off the debts, rented our apartment."

"What the fuck were they thinking?"

"They weren't. They'd never worked a day in their life and weren't required too."

Tank wanted to wipe the sadness from Elijah's beautiful face. He stepped away from the car and took Elijah's hands tugging him off the hood.

"Okay, how do I do this?" Elijah asked.

"Tank will get on, you'll settle in behind him and set your feet on the pegs. Move with Tank. Lean when he leans and all that shit. Just hang on, and he'll take care of you. Relax, this is supposed to be fun."

"Okay."

"Here, we got you this." Scary lifted the new helmet off the seat. "You can tell us what you want Tank to paint on it."

"Thank you."

Elijah softly spoke as Scary set the half-helmet with the tinted visor on his mop of curls. Scary secured the chin strap and leaned down to place a quick kiss on Elijah's lips that tilted into a small smile.

Tank swung his leg over the bike and settled into the seat, then he reached for Elijah's hand to help him swing up. His man settled in behind him, slim thighs lightly gripped his hips. Elijah's lean muscled arms twined around his waist.

"Let's get going," Scary bellowed as several bikes rumbled to life.

Elijah jumped a bit when Tank started his motorcycle, but eased and leaned against his back. He pulled into the lead beside Scary as they headed out of town. Elijah's long fingers gently stroked his stomach. It still shocked him someone would touch him gently or look at him with anything other than disgust when they saw his face and neck. Maybe he was finally going to get something good after all the hell he'd been through. If so, it was about fucking time.

♦ ♦ ♦

About three hours later they pulled off at an old-fashioned drive-thru and parked off to the side. He turned off his bike, leaned back into Elijah and then turned to cast his gaze along the line of bikes. Elijah slid his arms over Tank's shoulders and loosely hugged his neck. He almost flinched when Elijah dragged his lips the length of Tank's scar, and he closed his eyes tight at the unfamiliar sensation of his eyes burning.

"That was incredible. Thank you, Tank."

He reached back to stroke the underside of Elijah's thigh.

"Don't the two of you look fucking cozy," Scary's rumbling voice had them both looking up.

Tank still wasn't sure if Scary was okay with sharing. He was waiting for something to go down, and he'd lose the new set of emotions he was feeling. Admitting what it might be or would turn into scared the shit out of him. He already knew he was attached the beautiful man, and he was happy to share him with Scary, but his best friend wasn't one to play well with others. Over the years, he and Scary had butted heads enough to know sometimes their dominant personalities clashed.

"Princess is starved and isn't waiting for us." Scary tilted his head toward the small cement building, and Princess already stood in line giving them an impatient glare.

Elijah lifted on the pegs and swung one leg over to settle on the ground. He wobbled a bit, both he and Scary grabbed an arm to steady him.

"Takes a minute to get your legs back."

"I see that. I'm going to wait with Mi... Princess." Elijah rose on his toes barely reaching Scary's chin and quickly kissing the dark stubble.

They both turned to watch Elijah's sexy ass as he walked away.

"I can't wait to get my hands on that."

Tank grunted in agreement. *We need to take him on a date just us*—Tank signed. Group activities were to get Elijah used to the idea he was in a relationship with two damaged bastards. He knew for innocent Elijah going from barely dating anyone to involved with him and Scary had to be a huge leap of faith.

"Yeah, I was thinking about that on the way here. Next Saturday we can have him over to my house."

That would work—Tank glanced toward Elijah who now had Princess perched on his hip—*there is a lot we have to talk about.*

"Yeah, this baby steps bullshit isn't exactly our style, man."

Tank had to agree. They hadn't gotten where they were by dragging their feet. He tried to convince himself Elijah was worth taking it slow, but his gut told him if they took it too slow with their man he'd rethink being with them and make an excuse to escape. That wasn't fucking happening. Elijah Vaughn was theirs, and the sooner he realized it, the better.

"We better get over there and buy our boy lunch before he does it himself."

Tank nodded and dismounted from his bike. By next weekend their boy would know for sure, they weren't fucking around.

8 SCARY'S GOING AWAY FOR MURDER

Scary's huge fists clenched as he snarled at the three police cruisers lined up across the road from Brawlers. They loved to bust his and Tank's balls. Their pasts weren't squeaky clean, sometimes laws were meant to be bent, but to the cops around there being gay was enough to warrant a close watch.

Tank was inside taking care of an escalating issue which would end only one way, in a brawl. The guys were regulars, and they pulled this shit at least a few weekends a month. The anger bang must be worth busted lips and black eyes. The big guy's twink boyfriend liked to flirt, and Scary quickly realized he did it on purpose.

The rumor was the little guy got off on rough play. Scary was sure they could take care of their kink without fucking up his bar especially with the cops with a hard-on for staking them out.

He stepped forward and Crave grabbed his arm. "Be nice, boss."

"I'm always fucking nice."

"We'll start gathering a pool for bail money."

"Fuck you," Scary grunted and strode across the parking lot, then across the deserted road.

"Mr. Sheridan, what can we do for you tonight?" Officer Bastard smirked at him.

Scary resisted the urge to wipe the asphalt with his smug face. "Don't y'all have better shit to do than sit outside my place all night?"

"Just keeping the peace, sir."

"We can handle our own shit, Officer."

"I'm sure you can, but that's our job, not yours."

The beeping of his phone saved him from taking a swing. *I can't go to jail,* Scary kept repeating it as he checked his phone. A message from his bartender Twitch popped up. His petite bartender was worthless in a fight.

We've got three down. Need backup ASAP.

He cursed under his breath as he turned away from the cop and calmly made his way back to the bar.

"Something we can help you—"

Scary blocked him out as he made it to the doors and shoved them open. He swung at the first fucker who had the balls to come at him. Scary spotted Tank on the opposite side of the room. There was a man attached to his back, and he was exchanging blows with another.

"We don't get this under control, I got six assholes with badges ready to storm in," he hollered to be heard over the crowd as Crave came up on his right.

"I'll take the right, you go to the left, and maybe we can knock the fuck out of enough of them to get some attention."

"It's a plan." Scary pushed his huge body into the crowd.

Someone got in a sucker punch, and Scary tasted blood. He grabbed the guy's t-shirt and just as he was about to send the bastard sailing through the air the deafening clang of a gong froze everyone in place.

He jerked his attention to the door to find Elijah standing on the narrow counter running the length of the wall near the pool tables a bat in his hands. Scary still had his hands fisted in cotton, but he felt a smile pull at the corners of his mouth.

There stood his man in an expensive three-piece suit, his hair immaculate and looked around the room with a disgusted expression on his cute face. He'd be more pissed if he didn't see Crave guarding him.

"Now, I know there's overabundance of testosterone in this room. If no one wants to be arrested by six very upset police officers heading this way everyone better start acting like they have some sense."

Elijah motioned to Crave to be helped down, and Scary lost sight of him until the crowd started to part. When Elijah approached, he was shaking his head and pulling a handkerchief from his pocket.

"Lean down," Elijah ordered.

"My hero. Now, tell me why I shouldn't redden your ass for putting yourself in danger?"

"Crave was there, and as I've learned, law enforcement isn't among your biggest fans. I'd prefer not to have to go down there to bail you out."

He looked around to see everyone pretending they weren't fighting minutes before.

"Ain't that the fucking truth, can you imagine the gossip the mayor having to bail out one of his hoodlum boyfriends?"

"I don't care about that."

Scary let Elijah clean his busted lip all the while Elijah wore a disapproving expression. He didn't understand it, but he felt slightly guilty for disappointing Elijah. Oh fuck, this having a boyfriend thing was going to suck.

"Where's Tank?"

"Toward the back near the bar."

"Is he injured?"

"I don't know, let's go find out." He steered Elijah toward Tank when he noticed the cops walking in.

They looked pissed off as they were smiled at as the whole room waved at them. Scary snorted as he let Crave handle them. They broke through the crowd and Elijah ran right into Tank. The man instantly embraced Elijah.

"Look at you." Elijah leaned back and turned the cloth around to wipe at the cut above Tank's eye gently. A new scar bisecting the old one.

Sorry—Tank signed, but the grin on the man's face ruined it.

"Save it. You're like big kids."

"What are you doing here? You didn't call."

Elijah barely spared him a glance then turned back to finish cleaning the blood from Tank's face. "I didn't think I had to call to see you both."

"You don't, sorry, this nearly got out of fucking hand." Scary scanned the open room to find his customers lined up around the perimeter. The cops were trying to get answers, but no one was talking.

"I came by to let y'all know I have to cancel our date Saturday."

"Why, decided we're too much trouble?" Scary ignored Tank's glare.

"No, I, um, have a job interview and I have to go out of town."

"Where?"

"Atlanta."

"Why do you have a job interview? Someone giving you shit?"

"No, nothing like that. There's an LGBT Organization that needs a director. Housing, outreach and counseling for teens in crisis. It would mean some commuting, but I can work from home too."

"Are you giving up your job for us?"

"Maybe."

"Come with us." Scary took his hand and led him down the hallway toward the office. He nudged Elijah into the room and Tank closed the door behind them. "Explain."

"You're being difficult."

"Don't give a fuck, spill."

"When I ran for mayor I wanted to make a difference. I'm not exactly doing that. With the new job, I can. Now, part of the reason is—"

"Keep going."

"Fine, if we're going to make a go—"

"If?"

"You sound like Landon, do you have to keep interrupting me?"

"Start talking faster. I'm losing my patience."

"You're a pain. Listen, I don't understand why you two want to date me, but I'm willing to give it a try. To do that, I don't want to fight with the upper crust of this town. I'm not saying I'm quitting my job now. I still need to go to the interview Saturday afternoon. They wanted to get the entire board together.

"If I get the job, then I'll have to meet with the Town Council to give my resignation. They will appoint an interim mayor until a permanent replacement can be elected." Elijah leaned back against the desk. "I don't want to fight about this. It's not going to hurt my feelings to give up the job."

"We don't want to change your fucking life completely. We can deal with you being all proper and shit."

Elijah rolled his eyes and crossed his arms.

"What about you," Elijah asked Tank.

Whatever makes you happy. I do not want to turn your life upside down.—Tank shrugged and went to sit on the desk beside Elijah.

"You're not. Even if we don't work out. I want to do this."

"As long as we're not fucking up your plans."

"I promise. Now, I'm going home."

"You won't even stay for a drink?"

"I don't drink."

"Then coffee. You can't show up here and then just leave. Besides you're bailing on us for our date."

"Is this a guilt trip?"

Scary watched as Tank tapped Elijah on the shoulder and when the man turned to Tank all his friend did was nod.

"Fine, if you're both going to gang up on me."

"Thought so, but first, I think we've been patient."

"Wha—what—"

"You put yourself in a dangerous situation." Scary closed the short distance just as Tank lifted Elijah off the edge of the desk and placed him between Tank's muscular thighs.

Elijah leaned back against Tank's chest and tipped his head back. The slender column of his man's throat was exposed, and he leaned down to draw the edges of his teeth down Elijah's pounding pulse. His cock flexed at the submissive move as Elijah leaned his head to the side.

"You're sexy as fuck. Tank's going to take off your jacket."

Even as he said it, Scary leaned back to watch Tank remove their boy's coat, then his vest to expose the pale pink dress shirt. A glazed blue gaze watched him from beneath a thick fringe of dark lashes. He let his gaze travel downward to the bulge pushing at the front of gray pants.

Scary reached down to cup Elijah and squeezed, the man's slim hips jerked forward as Tank started to work on the buttons of Elijah's shirt. He focused on each inch of perfectly smooth skin exposed.

"Who do you belong to, boy," Scary growled.

Elijah's cheeks were tinged pink with what he knew was equal parts arousal and embarrassment. The last of the disks slipped free, and Tank pulled Elijah's shirt from his pants. His chest was flushed and his nipples hard.

"Answer me, every inch of you belongs to who?"

"I belong to y'all."

"Yes, you fucking do. Have you ever sucked a cock before, boy?"

"No—no."

"On your knees, boy."

He observed as Elijah trembled and stepped away from Tank, then slowly lowered to his knees. The smaller man roughly panted as Scary popped the button on his jeans and then slid down his zipper. He groaned as his calloused hand circled his dick, his palm and fingers catching on the bars of his Jacob's ladder that ran from the length of his shaft.

"Open your mouth," he ordered.

Elijah parted his plump pink lips, and he painted them with pre-come, he growled and jerked his hips at the tentative stroke of Elijah's tongue.

"Good boy," Scary praised Elijah and then he looked up to find Tank pushing at the thick bulge in his jeans. Tank's hungry, heated gaze peered down at Elijah. He understood, there wasn't anything sexier than their boy on his knees for them.

Tank stepped up until his feet straddled Elijah's calves. Elijah automatically reclined back against Tank's thighs, and Scary took another step to bring his cock back into contact with Elijah's mouth.

"We'll start slow, just suck the head and slide down, we'll work on your gag reflex later. Open."

Elijah obeyed perfectly and opened his mouth wide, wrapping his lips around the head. A rumble sounded deep in his chest at the gentle pressure and the ever so slow glide of wet heat suckling. "Perfect."

"Boss, Boss, we've got a problem out here." Crave's voice had him cursing.

"What the fuck do you want? It better be good. If not, I'm going away for murder tonight," he bellowed as he looked down to find Elijah with his forehead resting on his thigh and his face was scarlet.

"Um, probably not a good thing to say with the cops standing out here."

"We'll be out in a minute."

"Oh fuck, sorry, boss."

"You're gonna be. Tank, get him dressed and take him to the bar for his cup of coffee."

Tank nodded as he helped Elijah to his feet.

"I'm sorry." Scary leaned down and kissed Elijah gently. "Tank will take care of you while I talk to the fuckers and then I'll join you, okay?"

"Okay."

He tucked himself back into his jeans and winced as he eased the zipper up. As soon as he saw a badge, his hard-on would be gone. He made sure everything was put right, and Tank put himself between Elijah and the door. Scary unlocked the door and pulled it open.

"What?"

Crave lowered his eyes to the ground. "They want to talk to you for a few. I think the fuckers want to make a report." Crave whispered. The other man's eyes widened as he looked passed him to notice Tank and Elijah.

"Mind your own business."

"Whatever you say, boss."

Crave calling him boss pissed him the fuck off. He knew the man only did it for show. Scary turned to find the biggest asshole waiting at the end of the hall that opened into the main room. He pulled the door shut and headed in the cop's direction. The sooner he got this over with, the sooner he could get back to his boy.

9 ELIJAH'S SHOPPING TRIP FROM HELL

Elijah narrowed his eyes at Brody and Landon, the two of them were acting weird—weirder than usual which shouldn't be possible. They'd shown up at his house along with Lucky and said they were going shopping. He hadn't understood what that had to do with him because Brody knew he hated shopping with a passion. Elijah sipped his coffee as he walked between them a few blocks over from Twirled.

"Are we going to the shop?"

"No, Mina's hanging out with the guys and—"

Lucky bounced in front of him. "We're going to have so much fucking fun!" The gleam in the crazy man's eyes had him backing up.

"If he thinks it's fun, I'm going home."

"Stop, this is for your own good." Landon looped his arm through his and tugged him close to his side.

"What do you mean for my own good?"

"Well, you're about to take two massive dicks up the ass, you need toys!" Lucky couldn't have said it any louder if he tried.

"Lucky, calm down. Take a breath." Brody grabbed the shaking Lucky.

"But this is going to be…can you imagine the size of the plugs? It'll be like gag sizes, well, not gagging really, they'll be going up his…yeah, yeah, off-topic, but do you have a gag reflex?"

"I'm in hell. I'm having a nightmare."

A camera click had him jerking his gaze to Lucky. "I'm posting this, just gotta figure out the right hashtag. Do Scary and Tank have a—"

"I will kill you."

"No, you won't. Priest would die of longing for my company, and you'd have his death on your hands. I'm expendable, but my fucking bear is precious."

"Elijah, hear us out," Brody pleaded with him.

"This is embarrassing, can't we do this—"

"No, we're not buying you a plug online. We have to buy you a few. Last time I was at your house, I peeked."

"Brody, that's personal." Mortification caused his face to burn. Was he a serial killer in his past life because there must be a reason for deserving these people for friends.

"You haven't updated the treasure box in quite a while."

"There's nothing wrong with the go-to toys." He wasn't going to admit to the frequency of their use since Scary, and now Tank was in his life. It barely took the edge off his horniness especially not since the night at Scary's house and the office at Brawlers.

"But, Elijah, you haven't seen the monstrosities—"

Elijah turned bright red and averted his eyes.

"Elijah! You're holding out."

"Well, I am dating—I can't believe I'm dating two men, when did my life turn into a porno about tattooed bikers and the twink?"

"Now, Elijah, you are so not a twink, way too fucking old—past the twink prime," Lucky scoffed.

"How have you survived to the ripe old age of twenty-eight?"

"I'm cute and charming?"

"Like a rabid wolverine."

"You think I'm dangerous and ferocious. I like it."

"Only you'd take that as a compliment."

Lucky shrugged.

"You have a death wish."

"Well, it is at the end of my bucket list to have my obituary say that I died in the dildo aisle while screaming give me orgasms or give me death. Everyone has to have a goal."

"Ignore him." Landon stepped between him and Lucky. "You became one of us when Brody committed to this crazy ass crew of ours. As one of us, we want what's best for you. I've known Scary and Tank for a decade. And in that time, I've learned they're not the subtle or gentle types."

"But sex lives should be private. I'm not like y'all."

"Nothing wrong with that, but would you rather be proactive and prepare yourself—forgive the pun. There's no shame in this."

"But this is embarrassing, and you brought him," he whined and shot Lucky a death stare.

"I'm here for comic relief. I'm a fucking wealth of joy and hippie inspiration, motherfucker. Namaste and clean Chakras and all that good shit."

"You need heavy sedation, hell, you just need to be medicated."

Lucky started singing. It took him a moment, but then he realized the crazy shit was singing *Ramones I Wanna be Sedated*.

"There's something seriously wrong with you."

"Me, please, I am a well-adjusted member—" Lucky snorted. "I said member. I'm feeling all Victorian virgin he thrust—" Oh kill him now, the British accent was atrocious. "His throbbing mem—"

"Stop."

"I never understood that. Cock, what the fuck is wrong with cock? In my book, cock is best. It's throbbing, hard, thick or slender, cock is the way to go. Ride it, pound it into. Cock, cock, cock—" Brody, Landon and him slapped their hands over Lucky's mouth.

"If we're going to do this, can we just get it over before I go away for murder and I don't have to worry about new toys or if I'm ready for two mammoth boyfriends."

"Fuck yeah, let's do this damn thing." Lucky fist-pumped the air.

He squeaked as Lucky's arm slipped under his and practically dragged him through the door. Brody and Landon chuckled as they followed.

"Welcome to Plugs-R-Us, where all your stretching needs will be fulfilled before Scary and Tank plow you. Hey, Fred," Lucky called the guy behind the counter.

"Hey, twice in one week? Thought you had a pretty bear?"

Fred aimed a dubious glance his way.

"Oh no, this ain't mine, this belongs to two of—"

"Shut up, Lucky."

"Two, wow, innocent and freaky, why didn't you bring him around before?"

"Naw, man, he's obsessed with riding the massive—"

Lucky grunted as Elijah rammed his elbow into his chest. "I'll gladly go to prison before this day is over."

"Do you know how popular you'd be in prison? My asshole cringes at the thought."

Elijah adored Lucky, even if the man was completely and utterly insane, but his patience had a limit. He'd just reached it. "Let's make a deal, never mention your cringing asshole ever again."

"Prude. Fred, my good man, point us in the direction of the plugs."

"Straight back, third aisle over, you should know that by now."

"I don't come here that fucking often."

"Sure, man, whatever you say."

He dropped his chin to his chest and let Lucky lead him. This proved he needed new friends and to think he'd longed to be a part of this group. What had he been thinking?

"Okay, I'm assuming you don't have any plugs at home."

"No, why would I need one, I have a very—what in fake Jesus' name am I saying?"

"Loosen up, get it—loosen up."

"I'm so out of here." He spun to escape only to come face to face with Brody.

"Vagina up, man," Lucky ordered.

"What are you talking about?"

"I would say Nut up, but one tap to the nuts and the biggest and baddest goes down like a slut at a blowjob competition, a vagina shoots out a kid. What the fuck is that? That shit can take a fucking pounding, those things self-lube and instantaneous stretch. Lucky bitches. I've never tried one, but I'm sure Brody knows all about that shit."

"Don't you ever just stop and think, you know maybe I shouldn't say that?"

Lucky looked confused by the question. "No. My Mama said women are the stronger sex."

"I didn't think so, and I do love your mother." Lily Trenton like her son was a menace, but he loved her as much as he did Peaches.

"Yeah, everyone does, she's a goddess." Lucky approached the display and faced him. "Okay, back to the task at hand. It's kinda like getting your ears stretched, sometimes you want to just go for it, punch it or just shove that taper in like a motherfucking boss, but in this case gradual is key. Now, I'm more for a bit of burn," Lucky spoke as he waved his arm Vanna White style to a row of plugs in increasing sizes. "For you, my friend, we need to treat you like the delicate fucking flower you are."

Elijah felt his lips twitch and figured it finally happened the Twirled Crew drove him insane.

"So, big brother, this is what we're gonna do—"

"We?"

"We don't envy you," Landon and Brody said.

"My men are gorgeous."

"He said his men, and he's completely blind. Scary makes people cross the street to avoid him. I was one of them." Brody turned to check out the display of vibrators.

"But you have to admit him and Tank have that dangerous, bad boy thing going for them." Landon eyed a huge dildo shaped like a fist.

He shook his head and brought his attention back to Lucky.

"Start with this one first, wear it at work, it'll hit the prostate, and you'll be calling one or both of your men to come take care—"

"I'm not having office sex."

"I can attest that office sex is hot as hell. Zerk's come by a few times for lunch."

"You are all too free with telling people—" Another shutter of a camera drew his attention and he turned to find Lucky taking pictures of toys. "What are you doing?"

"Sending pics to Scary and Tank to ask what we should buy you?"

"What?" His voice rose several octaves as he started wringing his hands. Please let him be joking, he reached for his phone to start making flight reservations for Antarctica.

"Um, yeah, I mean, they're kinda for them too."

"I'm out of here. How many have you sent them?"

"I don't know, I've gotten a few texts, the language those two can pop out is fucking shocking. For a silent dude, Tank can sure get the point across through text."

"I'm going home now—" He turned to head for the door, and his worst nightmare happened. Tank and Scary were coming through the door, and the look on their faces was enough to scare the hell out of sociopath. "Oh hell." He ducked into the circular rack of fetish wear and sat in the middle of it.

"What the fuck are you three up to?" Scary's voice was gravelly and pissed.

"Scary, Tank, how are you two today?"

Elijah almost snorted at the sugary sweet and innocent tone Landon was trying to pull off.

"Don't use that bullshit tone, I've walked in on Zerk fucking you like you're goddamn Gumby. Where the fuck is our boy?"

"He was just here—"

"He's hiding in the rack."

Lucky that snitch. Elijah drew his knees to his chest and wished for invisibility. The plastic hangers clicked together as French Maid costumes parted and there were his men crouched down looking at him.

"How did you get into this?"

"They ambushed me. I thought we were going shopping. Lucky said since I was taking two—"

"Baby, come out of there."

Tank held out his hand.

"I don't wanna, I just want to live here. I could do a lot with this space."

Tank's lips twitched. *Please*—Tank signed. Scary disappeared.

He shook his head, Tank just smiled and crawled in with him. He laughed as Tank lifted him onto his lap and snuggled him close. His life wasn't boring since the Twirled Crew came into his life.

My heroes, thank you for saving me—Elijah signed. Tank responded with you're welcome. He laid his head on Tank's chest and waited for Scary to get the three annoying men to leave.

"You three can go, we'll take care of our boy from here. This was our fucking business and you three nosy shits should've stayed out of it."

"But, Scary, we've seen you naked, my brother doesn't need to feel like he's been fisted by Godzilla and now there's two of you. The sheer mechanics of it are mind-boggling. The porn is horrific."

He groaned as he covered his face and Tank chuckled at him.

"Out, we're fucking done with y'all."

"Can't we say—"

A growl cut Landon off.

"No, you can't. Say bye, I think you three have done enough damage. Now we gotta talk our boy out of living in a rack of fetish latex."

"But, but, Scary, I had a whole fucking tutorial planned. We were just getting to the gradual stretch and to start with—"

"I will kill you and make your dream of fucking your little bear impossible."

"Don't threaten my man's future transcendent sexual experience with this hot fucking hippie," Lucky grumbling faded as it appeared he was leaving.

It got quiet, and then Scary reappeared.

"The coast is clear. What the hell were you thinking?"

"That I was safe with my friend and brother, then Lucky showed up, and it spiraled out of control. Is he on drugs?"

"Prescribed or recreational?"

"Either because that man is insane."

"You want to know something fucking scary?"

"Don't tell me he's mellowed."

"Since Priest has been around, yeah. What are you doing here?"

"Dying of embarrassment. I was about to start checking for flights to Antarctica."

Tank chuckled loudly and tightened his arms around Elijah.

"Come on, let's buy you some new toys."

"No," Elijah squeaked.

"Yes, something we can watch you fuck yourself with later."

"You're as bad as them."

Tank lifted him and passed him to Scary, this having boyfriends much bigger than him was starting to suck.

Elijah straightened to find Fred watching them with an amused look on his face.

"Do I have to pick stuff out?"

"No, we fucking got this handled."

He stood back as his men had a silent conversation as they picked up several boxes and he followed behind. Every time he tried to peek at what they held they'd move shoulder to shoulder blocking him.

"What are y'all getting?"

"You'll see later when you come to the house for the date you rescheduled for some fucking job interview."

"Don't be mean."

"Not mean, honest."

He fell into silence as Tank led him toward the door while Scary headed for the register.

"What did you two get," he asked as he walked outside.

Tank shook his head.

He huffed and crossed his arms as he leaned back against the brick wall beside the door.

Quit pouting—Tank signed.

"I'm not pouting." He caught Tank rolling his eyes.

Tank closed the distance between them and braced his hands on either side of Elijah's head. His man leaned down, and Tank rubbed his scruff along his throat. He closed his eyes as he brought his hands up to settle on Tank's sides. The roughness of Tank's beard caused him to shiver. How did he make it to his age without realizing what he was missing?

Drawing back slightly until he could stroke his lips against Tank's and suck at his lower one, while Tank mirrored the move on Elijah's top lip. He didn't care they were in public. Elijah fisted his fingers in Tank's t-shirt and tugged him a little closer. Tank's hands sunk into his hair and pulled until Elijah's head tipped back to deepen the kiss.

His natural pessimism tried to take over, and he pushed it away. A relationship with these two men was what he wanted, and he didn't know where it would go, but he wasn't going to deny it to himself or anyone else.

10 TANK IS THE ODD MAN OUT

Organizing the receipts and taking care of the accounting for the night was the shit part of his job. Tank sipped his pint and tried to put away the fucked up direction of his thoughts. He admitted he wasn't the most confident fucker around. The scars kind of messed with his head for two decades. Guys like Elijah didn't fall into his lap. Scary didn't give a fuck what anyone thought and most days Tank didn't either, yet this was Elijah.

He opened the spreadsheet to start inputting the information he needed to send to their accountant for the morning. Tank looked around to make sure everyone had vacated the premises before he slipped on his reading glasses. Forty-three years of bar fights and security was taking its toll on him, he wasn't pretty—unlike Elijah.

Tank never met a man whose lips were so soft. Elijah touched his scars as if they didn't exist. He'd had plenty of men who wanted to bend over for him, but none who wanted to touch him—kiss him. It was a pathetic turn of events. It was almost laughable how hard he'd fallen. Scarred and cold, Tank Davis was close to caring for someone for the first time in twenty years.

He remembered the first one, the reason he'd come out of the closet and tattooed a target on his back. His neighborhood didn't tolerate differences. Gay got a guy's ass stomped into the asphalt. If you were lucky, you'd be able to crawl away, and if not, it was a one-way trip to the morgue.

Ian had been like him, big and rough, and in no hurry to have his ass six-feet under. They'd met up every chance they got at a motel as far from their home turf as possible. He knew they didn't love each other—he wasn't disillusioned enough to think at twenty-three he'd have anything permanent. The experience accomplished one thing he hadn't wanted to hide.

He'd packed up his shit and got ready to leave, Scary came by his apartment to ask him what the fuck he was doing. Back then Scary had been called Brawler. The most dangerous fucker in the neighborhood and Tank's best friend. He'd come out, and Scary nearly knocked his teeth out for keeping shit from him.

Tank informed Scary he was leaving town, but he needed to do one thing first. His best friend said he'd go home and pack, and they'd head out together.

He'd shown up at Ian's place, and it was going to be a simple goodbye. Word got around quick. Ian trying to save his own ass from the crew almost ended Tank's life. He could still feel the edge of Ian's knife as it split open his face. The kicks and punches from ten guys with Ian pushing them to hit harder. A fist had knotted in his hair and wrenched his head back, pain and adrenaline numbed the sting as skin split opening his throat.

The pain of broken bones and betrayal made his impending death much easier to accept. The last thing he'd remembered was the laughter and men spitting on him. He woke up days later with Scary beside his hospital bed.

At that moment, he'd shut down completely. The doctors said there wasn't any reason for him not to talk— the damage not severe enough to be permanent. He shook his head and looked down at the abandoned paperwork.

"I know that fucking look. Man, it never gets your oversized ass anywhere." Scary slid onto a barstool beside him. "Ian was a long fucking time ago."

Kind of a bitch to forget—Tank stroked his hand down the side of his face.

"Man, everyone has that one dick they'd pray or whatever to fucking forget. You gotta admit we got one helluva life now."

Tank stood and slipped behind the bar to pour Scary a pint and shot. He slid them toward Scary.

Elijah—he dropped his hands.

"Elijah, what?"

Does he want me or is it just to get you—Tank asked and realized his mistake at the rage in Scary's gaze.

"Don't pull that pity-me bullshit. Don't look right on a man your size. Elijah looks at that ugly mug just like he does me. The man has gotta have some major mental issues to fucking want us. We ain't exactly the prettiest to look at."

Tank grunted out a laugh.

We should break in and check his medicine cabinet—He reached for his pint and finished the contents in two gulps.

"I think security systems have changed since our B and E days."

True. Still—Tank raised a brow.

"Knock off the shit, fucker. We got a man. How the fuck did we end up sharing that sexy little man?"

Did I push—He stopped when Scary threw his hand up.

"You didn't push anything. Man, you should have seen your face the first time you saw Elijah. I thought you were gonna swallow your fucking tongue."

He touched my scars—Tank hated to admit it.

"If you don't wanna do this—"

Tank shook his head.

"Then what the fuck we gonna do? You know I don't want your hairy ass, right?"

You did not fucking say that—Tank signed horrified at the thought. At one time he hadn't been, his best friend was his first teenage crush. Back then the truth coming out terrified him and accepted the fact he needed to hide or die.

"Fuck, you should see your face."

Asshole—Tank rolled his eyes and poured them both a shot.

"Knock off the cold feet shit. We've already committed to this, and if we back out because you're an idiot, it'll hurt Elijah. I might be a bastard but I sure as fuck ain't hurting that man for the world. He's our boy whether we think we deserve him or not.

"We've fucked up enough over the years. Maybe it's about our time for some sort of redemption."

Tank swallowed the shot and went to pour another one when Scary swiped the bottle.

"No, no fucking drunk accounting. You know I can't fix that shit. Bruno still hasn't forgiven me for the last time I tried to do the books."

Tank snorted. He swore Bruno was crying the day after getting the paperwork from Scary and called Tank.

"You don't gotta be so fucking amused."

He shrugged and retook his seat to get the paperwork finished and fill out the deposit. Tank rechecked the receipts and cash, slipped the receipts in an envelope, the cash and deposit slip into the money bag.

Scary steadily took draws off his pint as his hand shot out and grabbed Tank's phone.

What the hell are you doing—Tank tried to get his phone back.

"I'm doing this for your own fucking good. Now shut up."

He rolled his eyes as Scary unlocked his phone. Scary hit speaker and set the phone down.

Elijah answered, "Hi, Tank."

"Hey, Elijah."

"Scary, what are you two doing at three a.m.?"

"Shit, forgot you normal people sleep."

"Hey, don't be mean. You weird people should be in bed."

"If you'd stuck your cute ass around here we would have taken you to one of our beds."

Do not embarrass him—Tank signed then pushed Scary.

"Tank thinks I'm making you blush."

"You are."

"I'm going to ask you a question, and you're gonna be fucking honest, got me?"

"Of course. Is everything okay?"

Now you are making him nervous—He didn't like the sound of Elijah's voice, and Scary was ignoring him.

"Tank's being a fucking idiot and thinking he's the odd man out."

"What—did I do something?"

"No, you didn't do a damn thing. Tank thinks we ain't equal in this shit."

"Oh, I mean I go from never having a boyfriend to having two. I'm still adjusting, but I thought we were—"

"We're doing fine. I told him you could deal with his ugly mug."

"Tank is not ugly."

He met Scary's eyes, and they smiled. There hadn't been much for them to be happy about in their lives, now they had a chance. He didn't want to fuck up, and he was so sure he was.

"When you headed back?"

"Right after the meeting tomorrow, I should be home about eight."

"Stay there, we'll head that way after we get up. Text us the address and leave a key at the front desk." Scary finally glanced at Tank, and he nodded in agreement.

"Really?"

"We'll take you out on a date. Maybe we'll be able to celebrate a new fucking job."

"Okay, I'll arrange everything. I need to get to sleep." Elijah yawned.

"Fine, you'll get used to our hours soon enough."

"I doubt it."

"Get to bed."

Tank waved, and Scary rolled his eyes. "Tank says good night."

"Good night, Tank, Scary. I'll see you both tonight. Be careful going home and heading this way." Elijah's voice was quiet but firm.

"We'll be fine, we've taken longer rides on Sundays."

"Yeah, yeah, my big bad men can take care of themselves."

"Quit pouting."

"I'm going to bed."

"Get some sleep; we have plans for you."

"Okay."

Scary disconnected the call. "Our boy is fucking fine. I'm headed home, you want me to take the deposit?"

Tank shook his head. He needed a long ride before he headed back to his cabin. Scary slapped him on the back and stood to head for the door. Gathering up the paperwork, he saved his work and closed his laptop, he took them back to the office to lock them in the safe. He slipped on his leather jacket, shoved the deposit bag in his backpack and shouldered it as he picked up his helmet.

Elijah was out, he'd kissed Tank on a public street, and he wouldn't be another Ian. He didn't have to pretend anymore and had a chance—finally something real. He set the alarm, locked the door and stepped out into the chilly night. Tank needed sleep, but like always it would well after dawn before he could close his eyes. The nightmares didn't come every night as before, but it still happened too often. He threw his leg over his bike and put on his helmet, securing the strap. Sleep would come soon enough, and then he'd be able to see his man.

11 ENTER THE JUVENILE DELINQUENT

Elijah didn't bother putting his suit jacket back on as he stood and looked across the cafeteria table at the Directors of the Center.

"Mr. Vaughn, it was a pleasure to meet you and thank you for agreeing to the weekend interview request." Kam smiled openly, and he'd instantly liked her when she'd greeted him. Her black hair mussed high on her head the magenta tips catching the overhead florescent lights. "We hope we didn't ruin any plans."

"It was an honor to be offered the interview. I had to reschedule a date, but they're meeting me here. They should already be at the hotel waiting."

"That was sweet of them to drive down."

Elijah could only smile. He hadn't expected Scary and Tank to pull a no-show at work on one of their busiest and roughest nights to come to him for their date.

"Well, we won't keep you, but we will say that your qualifications are exemplary and we look forward to working with you. As you provided all the information for the background checks that's one less step, we still need to finalize a few things such as a formal offer, but we will be in touch soon."

"Thank you so much." He said goodbye to everyone and then headed for the door. Elijah walked the maze of hallways that was once a schoolhouse that the board renovated for the Center. He stepped out into the bright sun and paused, the job offer almost finalized. He had a possible new job, boyfriends, a new life and he couldn't wait to start it.

He descended the steps and saw a thin figure beside the driver side of his car. They didn't look to be much taller than Mina. Stepping softly around his car he had a moment of shock to find whoever it was trying to use a Slim Jim to open the lock. Then he was amused by the creative use of the English language which would make any of the crew proud.

"You know it works better if you have the keys." He hit the button on the fob and watched a tanned, freckled face with huge, rounded eyes turn on him.

"Mister, you scared the fuck—"

"The name is Elijah, and you're far too young to cuss. Now, is there a reason you're attempting to start your life of crime at an exceptionally young age?"

"I'm twelve," she stated proudly.

"Almost old enough to be tried as an adult."

"You a cop?"

He bit the inside of his cheek to keep from laughing. It wasn't the time to be amused, but maybe the Twirled Crew finally warped his brain.

"Sophie, you were supposed to wait inside." Kam's voice kept him from answering. "Oh, Elijah, she wasn't bothering you, was she?"

He glanced at the juvenile delinquent and noticed her glare slash panicked look.

"No, she was very nice."

Kam sent him a look that said she thought he was insane or lying. Apparently, Sophie wasn't known for being nice.

"Your daughter is lovely."

"Thanks, but she's been placed with me until she can find a permanent home."

"Like that's gonna fucking—"

"Sophie, watch your mouth."

"She reminds me of someone." There was a mischievous glint in her eye that seemed too much like Lucky. He didn't think the world could take two of them.

"Her biological parents' rights were just terminated, and she's available for adoption, but her socialization skills are a bit—"

"She's like a feral child found in the woods after being raised by wolves."

"Pretty much," Kam agreed and snorted.

"I'm still here." Sophie's pout was almost too cute.

"She's not exactly putting her best face forward when we've met with potential adopters."

"Also, older children aren't as readily adopted."

"Sad fact. Come on, Sophie, we have to get home to figure out dinner."

"Will there be green stuff?"

"Children require vegetables to grow."

"Man, there ain't no more growing for me." Sophie stormed off with her thin arms crossed over her chest.

"Bye, Sophie."

"I hate that damn name," she mumbled at a stage whisper as she disappeared.

"Sorry for whatever she was about to do, my partner and I are at our wit's end. With her attitude, she wouldn't survive a group home, it would so go Lord of the Flies."

"I think she'll be just fine…be the total leader. She reminds me of my family back home, especially Lucky, he's mentally and physically incapable of not saying everything that comes to his mind."

"You must have a fascinating family."

"Most of them are family by choice, my parents died when I was eighteen and left me to raise my six-year-old brother. Not even a year ago, he fell for a tattooed heathen and his crew of misfits. They treat my niece like the Princess they nicknamed her."

"Your brother was very lucky to have you. I better get to her before I have to fork up bail."

"Completely understand."

He and Kam had exchanged quick goodbyes before she jogged off after Sophie. He opened his car door and slid into the driver's seat. Scary and Tank waited for him at the hotel, but his mind kept going back to Sophie. Over the years, he'd wondered what would've happened if he hadn't been able to raise Brody. How much would he have missed? Even today would he have known where Brody was?

He pushed the thoughts away. He'd raised Brody, been there for every milestone of his life, first days of school and plays, and everything in between. His GPS automatically retraced his trip back to the hotel. He wasn't entirely familiar with Atlanta but knew enough to get around.

Fifteen minutes later, he pulled into the parking garage and pulled into a spot near the elevator. Nerves started to dance in his stomach. Tonight wasn't the first time he'd been alone with Scary and Tank, although it was the only time they wouldn't be interrupted—just the three of them.

Being in a relationship with two men never crossed his mind, especially not men like his. They were the epitomes of bad boy, and he so wasn't. Hell, he'd never even had a parking ticket.

Sitting in his car all night wasn't going to get him anywhere, he had a date he'd waited a long time for. He got out, hit the alarm button and headed for the elevator. He'd found himself drawn to Scary from the moment he'd met him at Twirled World. Anything developing between them was simply a secret fantasy. The natural inclusion of Tank took him by surprise.

Tank and Scary both had shadows of their pasts always darkening their gazes. It naturally kept them apart from everyone else. He found himself resisting many times from smoothing the deep grooves between Scary's brows from his ever-present scowls. Also, kissing Tank's scars because even though Tank tensed when he touched them, something lightened about Tank's battle-ready stance.

He found himself stopping in front of his room so lost in his thoughts he hadn't realized he even reached his floor. He pulled the card key from his pocket, inserted the card until it beeped and he pushed the door open.

The scents of body wash and leather filled the room. Two sets of saddlebags rested beside his overnight bag near the dresser. Large leather jackets hung over the back of the couch. He closed the door with a soft click and stepped farther into the room. The balcony door stood open, Scary and Tank's large frames filled two patio chairs to overflowing.

He removed his tie as he went to join them and threw it to join their jackets.

"Been waiting long," he asked as he stepped through the open door.

"Couple of hours." Scary reached out to grab his wrist and pull him forward, Scary's chin tilted up.

He smiled and then kissed Scary's firm lips, what he meant to be a quick kiss turned instantly to an uncontrollable heat. Scary dominated his mouth—owned him. He couldn't protest because it was exactly what he needed. He needed their domination as much as Scary and Tank seemed to need his submission, he loved not being in control.

Suddenly he felt himself turned and pulled down onto Scary's lap, his back meeting the man's bare chest. Rough fingers began to work the buttons of his dress shirt free, and he watched as Tank loomed over him. Tank's large, rough hands holding his cheeks, then Tank leaned down but hesitated just before their mouth met.

"Hi," he whispered then closed the distance.

Scary and Tank appeared to be similar, but that was where their differences came into play. Where Scary took and owned him, Tank played him with a gentle dominance, yet possessed him just as deeply as his friend. Tank worked his mouth perfectly, thrusting, then nipping, teasing him until he could do no less than whimper.

He faintly felt his body jerk just before the afternoon breeze tantalizingly stroked over his sensitive bare skin. Scary spread his hands over his chest and pinched at his nipples—he arched into the slight pain. Tank thrust his fingers into Elijah's hair and tugged, just enough to cause his scalp to burn.

"After we've done this date thing all fucking proper." Scary nipped hard at his ear. "We're coming back here, and we're going to take that perfect ass. Do ya know why, boy?"

Tank gently eased the kiss, Elijah gasped for breath as he tried but failed to keep his hips still. The thick hard dick riding his crease caused his own to push at the zipper of his slacks.

"Why," he stuttered out as Tank lightly bit and sucked at his throat.

"Because you're ours."

Tank growled his agreement.

Elijah swore his heart just stopped. This didn't feel like a first date, it felt like a claiming—something permanent. His cynical side pleaded for him to deny it, but it couldn't because that was what he wanted.

"Say yes."

Those two simple words couldn't come across as anything other than an order.

"Yes."

Scary wrapped his hand roughly around Elijah's cock and stroked him through the layers of his pants and underwear. He jerked and moaned.

"Think about what we're going to do when we get you back here."

He shuddered in the circle of Scary's arms as Tank took his mouth in another rough kiss. Elijah didn't want it to end. He didn't want the date. All he needed was these two men. The way they didn't make him feel awkward or out of place. Elijah finally found the place he belonged.

12 MAKING LOVE WASN'T THEIR STYLE

Blood roared in his ears as Tank's heart picked up pace. He was waiting out front with Elijah while Scary took care of the bill. He had his arm thrown around Elijah's shoulder with the smaller man's head tucked beneath his chin. Elijah's arms loosely looped around his waist. He was unaccustomed to public displays, but it felt natural with Elijah. No one ever wanted—no he cut off that line of thought before it ruined his night.

"You're all tense, you okay?"

He just nodded because he didn't want to let Elijah go. Sometimes he wished he had the courage to try out his voice—to see if it was still there and the problem only existed in his head.

He turned as Scary exited the front door and tugged at his tie. He wasn't exactly faring any better with his, but the look of near lust and surprise on Elijah's face was worth it. They'd decided to do this shit right. Being someone's first time was a huge responsibility. The salesman did a double take earlier when they'd walked into the shop. With their size the fact they'd found anything to fit surprised them.

"Okay, how the fuck you do this suit and tie shit all the time freaks me out."

"It's not that bad, but—" Elijah turned but kept his back to Tank's as the smaller man reached out to grab Scary's tie. Elijah tugged at the silk tie until Scary approached. "You both look handsome."

"We're fucking taking this thing seriously, Elijah."

"Who would've thought the big and bad Scary Sheridan would be so sweet."

Tank snorted and wrapped his arms around Elijah as Scary growled. "You're asking for me to redden that sexy ass—"

"Elijah, isn't this a—surprise."

Tank turned to find two women and a little girl approaching, both the women's eyes were wide, but not as much as the tiny child. Her head tipped all the way back to stare up at Scary.

"Kam, let me introduce you, Scary and Tank this is Kam and her partner, I'm sorry, I'm Elijah." Elijah stepped away to shake hands with the other woman.

A lovely woman with long flowing blonde hair who looked as if she'd just walked off a magazine cover smiled. "I'm Megan."

"Megan, ladies, these are Scary Sheridan and Tank Davis."

"Nice to meet you, Ladies. Kam, you interviewed Elijah this afternoon?"

He shot Scary a glance at the almost friendly tone. He didn't think his best friend drank that fucking much tonight.

"Yes, and it was an extreme pleasure. We were just taking Sophie for ice cream."

He tapped Elijah's shoulder—*Tell them it is nice to meet them.* He hoped he wasn't going to embarrass Elijah in front of his prospective new boss.

"Tank says it's nice to meet you as well." Kam and Megan's faces and eyes lit up as they looked at him.

He did his best to smile politely and not look like he was grimacing in pain.

"How's your date going?"

"Perfect, we just finished dinner. Now, Sophie…" He noticed Elijah enunciated the girl's name, and Sophie rolled her eyes so hard he thought they were going to get stuck. "How's the life of crime coming for you?"

"I hate that damn name."

"Watch your mouth," Scary hissed out, and Sophie tensed, Tank didn't like that subtle move.

Elijah stood there with a grin on his face and pulled out his phone. "I have a niece your age, here," Elijah scrolled through his phone and pulled up a picture, then turned it toward Sophie.

"She has her ears pierced," Sophie squeaked in indignation. "Look at her hair." She grabbed Elijah's hands and thrust them toward Kam and Megan.

"I was thinking, Kam, why don't you two visit and bring Sophie, let her spend a little time with Mina—"

"Princess."

"Princess, sorry, everyone gets nicknames." Elijah turned his attention back to Sophie. "You can meet Princess and the rest of the crew."

He noticed Sophie wasn't looking at Elijah but at the phone. "She's really pretty. Her mom and dad let her do that to her hair?"

If he hadn't been paying attention, he wouldn't have seen the few seconds the miniature bad ass had disappeared before the growl and attitude fell back into place.

"Well, her Uncle Lucky took her to the park, and she came back like that, but her dad and papa agreed to the pierced ears. Her papa Trouble did them a few weeks ago."

"Did they let her keep her hair?"

"Yeah, she loves it, and it's not hurting anything. Self-expression is crucial."

"Actually, do either of you ride?" Scary's voice brought Tank's attention to his friend.

"We haven't been out in a long time, not a lot of time with work and life."

"The crew and us go out every Sunday, start early, get some lunch, back to the house for dinner. I think the Juvenile Delinquent in training might need some social skills."

"Listen, you—"

Scary knelt onto one knee to put them on eye level. "Yes?"

"I don't like you." Sophie's tiny fists tightened.

"I don't like you either."

"Sophia," Kam quietly admonished Sophie. "I'm so sorry." Kam reached out and grabbed Sophie's thin shoulders, but the little girl shook her off to continue to glare right in Scary's face.

Tank watched Sophie and Scary with more amusement than it warranted. Elijah returned to him and leaned back against him, he lowered his head to check

Elijah's expression. The smaller man watched Scary and Sophie with a smile that almost seemed content.

"We should get going, thank you for the offer—"

"Elijah will give you the address. Plan for next Sunday." Scary stood and picked up a protesting Sophie. "We're going to get ice cream."

Tank watched as Scary and Sophie headed down the block arguing. The girl did have a creative grasp of language. Elijah twined his fingers with his, and they followed with Kam and Megan beside them.

"Shouldn't they have a referee?" Megan asked.

"I think Sophie—"

"We need to give her a new name," Scary called over his shoulder. "She's on her way to Juvie at some point, how about that?"

Terrible name—Tank signed.

"But fitting," Elijah quipped.

"You and your men are weird," Kam said with a laugh. "Ever thought about having kids?"

"Don't even think about it, Elijah. I've got enough trouble with you."

Tank gravelly chuckled at Scary's menacing glare. They reached a small ice cream shop a few blocks away, and Tank sat back to observe. He'd never thought about the whole family thing. He had friends who were as close as brothers and Princess, a niece, but what did he know about belonging to a family group: Nothing. He was just getting used to his first boyfriend who saw him beyond the scars and silence.

Where would he fit within a unit where he shared his boyfriend? If one day Elijah wanted children would he be able to be a dad? He still didn't know to keep Elijah happy.

Two hours later they arrived back at the hotel, and he closed the door. Scary walked across the room and turned on the bedside lamp bathing the room in soft light. Tank reached out and removed Elijah's jacket, exposing the pale blue button up perfectly tailored to Elijah's slim shoulders. Elijah turned toward him, the smaller man nibbled nervously at his lower lip as Elijah raised his hands to push Tank's jacket off his shoulders.

Once his hands were free, he lifted them—*beautiful.*

"So are you," Elijah whispered. He raised his hands and curved them around the back of Tank's neck to pull him down.

Instead of going for his lips as he expected, Elijah's mouth traced his scars, each one, even the ugliest. Elijah's nose nudged his bearded chin until he titled his head back. Elijah licked along the jagged, raised skin and sucked lightly. His dick hardened, and he grabbed Elijah's trim waist to roughly tug him closer.

The subtle scent of soap and shampoo, the softness of Elijah's hair against his skin, and it had been so long since he'd been touched—loved, but he didn't think he'd ever been that.

He stroked his hands around to Elijah's back, over the curve of his perfect ass until he palmed the curves and lifted Elijah high onto his chest. Elijah's leanly muscled legs twined around his waist. Even with the need intensifying, Elijah kept his caresses and nips gentle—almost tender. He didn't want tender. He rumbled deep in his chest as he fisted his right hand in Elijah's curls and jerked his head back. Heavy-lidded blue eyes met his and the sweetest whimper passed Elijah's full lips. He slammed his mouth down onto Elijah's and walked toward the bed where Scary waited.

He noticed Scary had stripped down to his boxer briefs. Scary moved to the side so that he could lower Elijah to the bed. He thrust his tongue as his hips ground against Elijah's, feeling the smaller man's hard cock against his own. Fuck, he'd never wanted inside someone so fucking bad in his life. He lifted to his knees and dragged his lips along Elijah's jaw, down the side of his throat. Tank fisted his hands in Elijah's shirt and ripped it open.

Smooth, creamy skin glowed in the faint light. Tank canted his eyes up as Elijah groaned and found Scary kissing their man. Elijah's thighs tightened against his sides and Tank opened his mouth over a tight, pale tan nipple. He sucked and bit as Elijah's gorgeous body writhed under him.

He impatiently worked Elijah's belt, button and zipper until he gripped the side of Elijah's pants and underwear. Straightening, his chest ached from his ragged breaths, and he efficiently stripped Elijah until he wore nothing but the ruined dress shirt.

"Fuck, look at that." Scary stroked his hand down Elijah's chest, flat abdomen until he took Elijah's slender cock into his large hand.

A part of Tank waited for jealousy, but it never came.

"Suck our boy off and get him ready," Scary growled.

Tank watched Elijah, his body flushed a pale pink, and his cock steadily dripped pre-come as Scary stroked him. He eased off the bed, removed his clothes and not caring when he heard a few buttons rip. He kicked his shoes and pants aside, leaned down to jerk off his socks. Tank straightened and circled his cock, he took in Elijah's spread thighs and the sparse hair around his tight little hole. He wanted to split that ass wide; fuck Elijah until the man felt him for fucking days.

"Look at him, baby," Scary whispered next to Elijah's ear, and the slim man obeyed. "Ya want it don't ya, that fat cock tearing you apart, both our cocks pounding into you. Say it," Scary growled.

"Yes, please."

"Tank's taking that ass first, and then I am, after tonight ya ain't belonging to anyone else. Do ya understand? No one touches what's ours."

"Y-Yes."

It was all Scary and he needed to hear, he bent to pull the supplies from under the pillow where Scary stashed them earlier. He quickly ripped open the condom and rolled it on, before he dropped to his knees beside the bed. Tank reached out, wrapped his hands around Elijah's thighs and jerked him to the edge. He took Elijah's dick in one hand and swallowed it to the back of his throat in one hard thrust. Elijah dug his heels into the back of his shoulders.

"Too—too much." Elijah's voice rose with desperation.

"No, baby, ya can take it, watch how much he loves sucking your cock."

He looked up at Elijah as he bobbed up and down the shaft, retreated and hesitated long enough to tongue the slit gathering Elijah's taste to savor before plunging again. Elijah's eyes were bright and filled with lust as Tank held his gaze.

Reaching for the lube, he slicked his fingertips and brought them to the wrinkled, convulsing hole that was begging for him. He massaged and pushed, he showed no mercy as he breached Elijah with two thick fingers.

Elijah cried out and threw his head back. Scary bit at Elijah's ear, throat and along his jaw. "Relax, push out, let him in."

Scary met his gaze asking silently, and Tank felt Elijah relax, he slowly finger fucked him, scissoring until he released Elijah's cock and surged onto the bed. Scary dragged a shaking and whimpering Elijah farther up the mattress. Elijah's arm twined around their necks, Scary kissed him first, then Tank. He couldn't fucking wait, he grunted as he worked a third finger in and Elijah's hips jerked as he slammed down on them.

His skin felt on fire, his every muscle tensed to the breaking point and Tank could take no more. He pulled his fingers from Elijah's tight, gripping heat, slicked his covered cock with more slick and stroked down circling the base as he pressed the fat head to Elijah's ass. He looked down to meet Elijah's eyes, waited for some sign. That's when Elijah curled upward until his mouth touched Tank's.

"Please, so emp—"

He didn't wait for Elijah to finish before he thrust once until he was balls deep. Elijah screamed and lifted his ass off the mattress, shuddered breaths warmed Tank's lips. His man shook all over and clenched rhythmically around him. It was pure fucking torture as he waited, giving Elijah a minute.

"Ya ready, fuck, ya should see how your sweet fucking hole is spread wide."

Watery blue eyes still filled with desire stared into his and Elijah nodded sharply. Tank pulled out, then pushed back in, building the intensity of his pounding until high, grunts broke through the veil of the lust burning through his veins. Elijah's hard dick slapped between their bellies as

Tank realized he was Elijah's first—something primal and dangerous bloomed in his chest.

He lowered to his forearms, slipped his hands under Elijah to curve his hands around Elijah's shoulders. He claimed Elijah's mouth, eating every sweet cry and curse. At the edge of his mind his sensed Scary getting up, but he was too focused on his need to stake his part of the dual ownership, and they owned Elijah—every inch.

He flipped Elijah so the man was on top, placing his feet flat as he pounded, his balls drawing up tight and he froze as his orgasm brutally took him. His hips erratically moved as he pumped his seed into the condom. Loathing that he couldn't watch it turn Elijah's ass and thighs slick. He reached down quickly and held the condom as he eased out so Scary could take his place.

Looking passed Elijah's shoulder, he watched his best friend place his knees on the bed. The lines of Scary's face were harsher than normal. Scary's hairy calves brushed his thighs and then the larger man was blanketing Elijah's body. The first thrust arched Elijah's back. Tank was helpless as he watched Elijah's mouth fall open, his eyes squeezed tight, and Tank wrapped his hand around Elijah's weeping dick.

"Ours, boy, always." Scary grunted against the side of Elijah's throat before Scary latched onto Elijah's shoulder and bit down.

Scary rode their bodies hard and fast, Elijah froze, screamed and hot jets of seed painted Tank's hairy stomach as Scary threw his head back.

Tank had never seen a man more beautiful than Elijah, and he was theirs. Scary rolled to the side taking Elijah with him. Elijah whined as Scary moved away breaking contact.

They laid there lost in the quiet only broken by ragged breaths and thoughts all their own. Tank turned and gently kissed Elijah, felt the man sleepily respond. He smiled as he leaned back to see the content look on his man's face and his eyes were already closing.

He grunted to get Scary's attention and his best friend met his gaze.

I will clean him up. Be right back—Tank signed and rolled from the bed to head for the bathroom.

He stared in the mirror something he avoided most days, and for once he didn't see the haunted expression— the defeat.

Quickly, he cleaned up, grabbed what he needed for Elijah before heading back into the bedroom. Tank paused for a moment to watch Scary, and their man curled up on the bed, Elijah tucked into Scary's side. Elijah's eyes opened, the slender man smiled and patted the empty spot in front of him. Fuck, how the hell did he get so lucky? Maybe Scary was right, and it was their time for redemption. He hoped so and that it wasn't some fluke, but he'd worry about that later. Right then, his man waited for him.

13 THE MORNING AFTER AND MOMENT OF TRUTH

Scary groaned as he pulled the pillow over his head to block out the morning sun streaming through the balcony doors. They'd forgotten to close the curtains before they went to bed. His mouth pulled into a half-smile as the slender body curled up to his back. He turned to glance over his shoulder and saw Tank completely wrapped around Elijah, Elijah's forehead was pressed between Scary's shoulder blades. Tossing the pillow over the side of the bed, he rolled over to watch Elijah sleep.

Elijah's curls tangled around his face and dark lashes laid on his high cheekbones. The man was fucking beautiful. He wondered what the hell he and Tank did right. Scary lifted his hand, put his palm on Elijah's cheek and traced the long, fringe of lashes with the pad of his thumb. Elijah hummed in his sleep and turned into his touch, brushing a gentle kiss to his palm.

He'd noticed the tenderness with which he'd treated Tank, and it wasn't the first time he noticed. Elijah took advantage of every opportunity to touch them. It was an odd thing. No one touched either of them with anything close to reverence. Elijah wore his heart on his sleeve, and he damn sure couldn't disguise what he felt.

Scary was born to a single mother who worked her ass off to just put food on the table most nights. Monica barely turned seventeen before Scary made his way into the world. She'd been beautiful with rich, caramel colored skin and always laughing hazel eyes. No matter how tired his mom was, she wore a permanent smile. The man who knocked his mother up was rich and popular, a college boy who'd talked all sweet, but hadn't stuck around long.

He didn't give a fuck where the bastard was, but he wished his mom could've met Elijah. Breast cancer took her before her fortieth birthday. Monica would've approved of Elijah. She'd always said he'd need a good man to keep him in line. He'd never been in the closet with her, and she'd hated the necessity of keeping it quiet. His best friend hadn't known until the night they'd decided to leave the neighborhood behind. Neither of them had a reason to stay.

His life went into freefall after his mother died. Part of him hadn't cared whether he lived or died.

He dropped his hand from Elijah's face. The memory of his ex came back. Callum was gorgeous with a penchant for slumming on the weekends. He hadn't minded the occasional hookup, a hard fuck, and a quicker goodbye until it turned into something else. It hadn't been love, in his mid-twenties, he wasn't looking for permanent—well at least he hadn't thought he was.

Callum liked to tell his friends about the bad boy biker/tattoo artist. After a few years, it started to feel as if he'd turned into some exotic fucking pet. Callum always talked about taking him home to meet the parents. Later he came to find out Callum had a man who was just as pretty and rich. He refused to recall that last fight. It was his first and last heartbreak.

"You're frowning." Elijah sleepy voice broke into his thoughts.

"Isn't that normal for me?"

"Pretty much."

"Thanks."

"You're welcome. What were you thinking about?"

"An ex."

"From that tone, it wasn't a good experience."

"He was all upper class and privileged, and it turned out I was some taboo fuck...a weird status symbol."

"What an asshole."

Slender hands rubbed over his chest hair and a single finger dragged over one of his pierced nipples. He growled as the sharp tug sent pleasure coursing straight to his already perked up dick. As much as he wanted to fuck Elijah again, he knew his man needed a bit of time.

"I knew it at the time, but it was the first out of the closet thing I had." He leaned forward and sucked at Elijah's plump bottom lip. He bit down and listened to Elijah's sexy, little moan. He backed off before his control slipped. When it came to Elijah, he'd held back so long, he didn't want to anymore.

"This is my first."

"Why the fuck is that? You're gorgeous, intelligent and successful. Why the fuck did you wait?"

"Out of habit."

"Explain."

"Brody was mine from the day he came home from the hospital and being out in my school wasn't heard of, even if you knew which guys were hooking up. I spent nights feeding and putting a kid to bed then it was time for homework." Elijah laid his hand on his waist and flexed. Scary got the idea and moved closer until Elijah snuggled between him and Tank.

"When our parents died, I was supposed to head off to college, but I was staying local because I still had a kid. Awkward when you get asked out on a date and have to explain you can't find a babysitter, even weirder when you're only sixteen. Whether it was my choice or not, and to be honest, it was my choice. I took over, but when my peers were out drinking and partying, I was reading bedtime stories, trying to budget to make sure we'd afford groceries after all the bills were paid."

"That's a lot of responsibility for a kid, Elijah."

"I know." Elijah sighed. "But there wasn't anyone else."

He looked up to find Tank's eyes open, their gazes met, but Tank kept still as he listened.

"Then when Brody started school, I worked all day, took care of him in the evening and took night and online classes. There was this great elderly lady who lived in our building. She watched him the nights I went to class. So you see, all I could do was work my ass off to survive and make sure Brody thrived. Then when he got older and independent, my life was a habit. The dates I went on, the guys weren't established or had goals. I'm not saying going out most nights and weekends partying is a bad thing, but that isn't how I grew up. I became a father figure to my infant brother when I was twelve."

"Brody's grown with a daughter."

"Yeah, but—"

"But what."

"I spotted you the night we went to the shop. You were handsome and off-limits. You hated me, and I was pathetic."

"Really?" Elijah was attracted to him, he'd known it, but his prejudice kept him from doing anything about it. "I'm an asshole."

"Yeah, but you're a hot one."

"What about Tank?"

"Oh man, I looked at him, and it was just like with you. I thought I was some freak. I was instantly on edge. To find out I could have you both, excited and frightened me, still does."

"Why?"

"Because I'm not sure I'm enough. I'm boring. I've always thought I was okay looking."

"Fishing for compliments."

"No."

He knew that. There wasn't an ounce of artifice to the man. Elijah was exactly what he seemed. "Full disclosure, we don't think we're enough either."

"We make a weird trio."

Scary chuckled and leaned in for another kiss. "Yes, we do."

"So, what are we doing?"

"Well, we're dating and you ain't going anywhere."

"Wasn't planning on it."

"But what we're going to do now, you're going to make a phone call to the front desk and extend our stay another night, then you're calling in sick to work."

"Really, that's what I'm going to do?"

Elijah's raised brow and annoyed tone didn't fool him. The man didn't take orders from anyone, but when it came to him and Tank, Scary knew Elijah didn't want to be in control all the time.

"Yes, because Tank and me aren't ready to share, the guys will be all over us."

"I'm surprised my phone isn't going off."

"I turned it off before we went to sleep."

"Sneaky, Mr. Sheridan."

"Maybe." Scary rolled to his back, grabbed the phone and hit zero for the front desk. "Do as I say."

"Yes, sir." Elijah took the phone. "Yes, this is Mr. Vaughn, I wanted to stay another night." There was a pause. "Thank you. Yes, I'll be leaving tomorrow. Have a great day." Elijah handed over the phone.

He passed Elijah his cell phone. "Now, work."

"I'll call my assistant." Elijah squirmed until he was on his back. Elijah gave Tank a quick kiss and a good morning as he scrolled through his contacts. Elijah pressed the phone to his ear and waited. "Hi, Martha—no, everything is fine. I'm just going to be stuck in Atlanta until tomorrow. I'm going to need you to reschedule any appointments I have—Yes, I'll be back on Tuesday. Thank you, you're the best." After a few more things had been cleared up, Elijah disconnected the call. "Happy?"

"Extremely."

"Now, what are we going to do with another night of alone time?"

"We've got plans for you, but first we're going to head out to get breakfast and play it by ear from there. We were a little rougher on you last night than we planned, but we ain't exactly the gentle types."

"I wasn't complaining."

"We didn't think you were. Now, I'm going to shower, you and Tank do your own thing." He leaned over Elijah and took his mouth in a possessive kiss, he broke it again before he took things too far. He rolled from the bed and padded to the bathroom. Stopping at the door, he turned to watch Tank signing and Elijah talking quietly. His best friend and Elijah looked good together. He turned away and entered the room, he walked toward the large, shower stall and reached in to turn the taps.

He was happy for Tank—he was just fucking happy. Which was odd for him to realize that for the first time in twenty years, he was right where he wanted to be in life. He hadn't anticipated sharing a partner with his best friend. Something that could've been awkward was natural. He couldn't admit it yet, but he was falling fucking hard for Elijah, and he knew Tank was on the same page. One day maybe they could think about permanent, say it aloud, but for now, there was so much left to learn.

He entered the shower and leisurely scrubbed as he let the water run over his body. Tank and Elijah needed time alone, there was no doubt they'd share him, but one-on-one time would be important too. Sharing had never been his strong suit, but he'd learn—hopefully.

14 JUVIE MEETS THE CREW

The scent of fresh cut grass and strong coffee relaxed his tensed muscles, Elijah leaned back into the V of Tank's legs as they waited for Sophie, Kam and Megan to arrive. He didn't know why he was so nervous. They'd emailed him the official offer for him to take the job and he hadn't hesitated to accept. So his new job was a done deal. That should have been some weight lifted from his shoulders, but over the course of the week, he'd discovered he was more nervous whether Juvie would like the guys or not.

With the job offer, he'd drawn up his resignation papers and work turned into a nightmare. He hadn't been able to spend any time with Scary and Tank—no sleepovers. Two amazing days of just the three of them, but then they'd returned to reality which was his job and Brawlers for them. Their opposite schedules were going to be an adjustment. He woke up to texts every morning letting him know that they'd arrived home. When he was getting up, Scary and Tank had probably only been in a bed a few hours.

Tank's arms tightened around him, and his beard tickled the sensitive side of his neck. He loved the course beard brushing against his skin—he didn't care where. He lifted his right hand and wrapped it around Tank's thick, veined forearm.

"I know, I'm tense. Sorry." Elijah tuned into Tank on a level where words or signs weren't needed.

Scary approached and crouched down in front of him. "Juvie—"

Tank grunted at the nickname Scary bestowed on Sophie. It was terrible, but his opinion was still the same—it fit.

Scary continued as if Tank never protested. "Will be here soon."

"Why am I nervous?"

"You know why you're nervous, you're just too chicken shit to admit it to yourself." Scary spun to sit on the bottom step between his legs.

He kissed the top of Scary's shaved head. The stubble was slightly coarse against his lips.

"What are you talking—"

"You want to adopt her."

"I can't do that, what the hell would I do with a kid?"

"Same as you did with Brody, raise her to be amazing. You did a damn fine job with Brody."

He lowered his head. He wasn't great with compliments. He turned awkward and shy every time he received one, especially when it came from Scary or Tank, and they did it a lot.

"It's just not me, there's—"

"Don't try to fucking use us as an excuse. You want it bad enough then do it. Package deal or not, Tank and me are in this."

"I don't know, I haven't actively thought about it. And I've only seen her two times."

"But you have thought about it, and you do seem to have a thing for criminals."

"Maybe," he admitted, and Tank roughly chuckled behind him. "It's not exactly going to be easy."

"We've met her. We'll set up a nice little bail fund." Scary leaned his head back against his chest.

That was becoming his favorite place to be, sandwiched between his two large men. He'd quickly discovered they always took up protective positions on either side of him. Ready to step in at the smallest threat. It was nice. No one ever wanted to protect him before.

"She'd kinda fit in, wouldn't she?"

Tank signed yes beside him, and Scary grunted, it seemed to be answer enough. They hadn't told Mina someone new would be coming to meet her because they hadn't wanted to disappoint her if plans changed. So right then, she was laid back in her sidecar attached to Trouble's bike reading a book. Trouble and Brody were in the bed of Trouble's truck taking a nap before the ride.

Lucky and Priest, Zerk and Landon were lounging in lawn chairs downing coffee at alarming rates. These people were his family—every weird one of them, and he had to admit he loved them all, including Tank and Scary, but that's the one he couldn't admit aloud.

The sound of a motorcycle approaching broke into their conversation. He jerked his head up as a cute hybrid car pulled in right before the bike. He recognized Kam before she even took her helmet off. The back door open and the hoodie-wearing Sophie slunk out of the seat.

"Boys, check the valuables, the con's here," Scary shouted before he surged to his feet and reached back for his hand.

Scary tugged him to his feet and Tank followed as they approached the car with a brooding Sophie glaring at Scary with her arms crossed. If looks could kill Scary would be dead.

"Oh, hi," Mina squealed in her usual fashion and jumped from the sidecar. "I'm Princess." She was bouncing on her toes.

She was a hugger, but they'd had to talk to her about asking first and respecting personal space—hers as well as others.

Sophie was staring at Mina like she was an alien, but he noticed Sophie was twisting a lock of her long dark hair as she looked at Mina's with its bright wraps and braids. She dressed the same as the last time he'd seen her. Dark gray hoodie, baggy jeans and scuffed sneakers while Mina wore a flowing pale pink hippie shirt under a black leather jacket, ripped jeans and her small black combat boots.

"That's Juvie, Princess, we're going to need to work on her rudeness."

"You talking about being rude, Scary, you drink too much—"

Scary swiped at Lucky, but the man sidestepped the move quickly.

"If looks could kill, man, I like her already, she ain't a fan of yours. I'm Lucky, and this is my pretty bear, Priest."

"Lucky, behave."

He couldn't understand how the man dealt with Lucky on most days. He'd quickly considered Priest in line for sainthood.

Zerk and Landon introduced themselves. And he reintroduced everyone to Kam and Megan who were just staring at all the guys wide-eyed. He understood the feeling. He'd felt and looked the same the first time he'd met them a year before. Had it only been a year? It felt like so much longer.

He noticed Scary lean down and whisper something to Mina sending her running toward the house.

"Okay, here's the plan, Juvie's with me, Elijah's with Tank, everyone else takes their usual positions."

"Oh, I don't know, Sophie doesn't have—"

"Here, Uncle Scary." Mina skidded to a stop. "Can I give it to her, please?"

"Sure."

"Here." Mina held out the box.

"What is it," Sophie suspiciously asked as she watched the box like it would explode at any moment.

He was curious too, Scary hadn't mentioned getting Sophie anything, neither had Tank.

"Ya gotta open it, sort of the concept of a present." Lucky shifted as if it was a present for him.

The man was too easily excited. Again, he was nominating Priest for sainthood.

"Oh, you got—"

"Say thank you and open the box," Scary ordered, and it earned him another glare.

Mina kept hold of the box as Sophie ripped open the black paper with hot pink skulls. She lifted the lid, and a small gasp had him freezing.

"It's from Elijah, Tank and me, gotta have the right gear. You'll have to tell Tank what you want painted on your helmet. He'll have it ready for next time. Got your jacket a little big, but figured you got a bit of growing to do. Didn't know your shoe size, so boots will have to wait."

He slipped his arms around Scary's and gave it a squeeze.

"Okay, gear up we're burning daylight."

"Thanks." Sophie's voice was unnaturally quiet as she held the small jacket and her new helmet to her chest. She was rubbing the leather like a security blanket.

"Welcome. I've been riding since before I had a license. She's old enough to ride behind me I checked the laws."

"If she says it's okay, then we're okay with it," Kam said giving Sophie an option.

He noticed the smiles on both the women's faces. He could practically see the plotting going on. It was true he wanted to see about adopting Sophie. The biggest things holding him back were Scary and Tank, both put those worries to rest, but could he turn all four of them into a family unit. His two men never mentioned kids not even in casual conversation. They were amazing with Mina, but that was a niece who wasn't around twenty-four-seven. They could spoil and send her home. Sophie would be a lifetime commitment, and they hadn't even discussed their relationship being permanent even though the two men seemed as invested in their lives together like him. It was all so damn confusing.

"Okay."

"Here, let me help you with your helmet."

Elijah let Scary go as he knelt in front of Sophie.

"Lucky, ya gotta do my hair." Mina hopped over to Lucky.

Lucky quickly French braided Mina's long hair so it wouldn't get tangled on the ride.

"Could he do—"

"Got you covered, Juvie," Lucky absently said as he finished with Mina and stepped behind Sophie tugging her hood off. "We gotta do something about this. No individuality."

"Ask before you do anything to her hair," Priest muttered as he wandered off toward his bike.

"I was gonna."

Lucky so wasn't going to ask. He took cool uncle status seriously, and he strove to be the coolest. "I'll need her sizes. She needs clothes."

"I have clothes."

Lucky ignored her, and he had to laugh. "No skirts, she seems like she'd burn a skirt if I gave her one. I make kick ass clothes, you'll see." Lucky finished with her hair and tied it off with one of the leather straps he kept around his wrist for Mina and his hair.

"Let's go." Scary held his hand out to Sophie, and she stared at it before she took it carefully.

He hated what he was noticing. He'd taken a few things from the other night. She seemed to pull into herself and try to make herself as small as possible. The flinching was the biggest one. He never wanted her to feel the need to protect herself again.

She will be okay—Tank's hands moved gracefully—*we have this covered.*

I do not like her frightened—He replied wanting to keep their conversation private.

Do we look like we cannot handle what comes—Tank asked.

His answer was a snort and earned him a tight hug and a rough kiss. Tank walked off to help Scary get Sophie ready for the ride.

"You have those two men wrapped around your finger, you know that right," Kam asked as she stepped to his side with her arm wrapped around Megan's waist.

"I think it's the other way around."

"For all the frightening bad boy exteriors, they seem like really great guys—all of them." That was Megan.

"Family and all that, sometimes you choose the best ones." He looked around at the guys that roamed the front yard getting ready to ride out.

"You want to discuss something with me," Kam asked.

"I've thought about it. I raised Brody, I know the procedures, the visits, and I know it'll be hard because I'm gay."

"Elijah, I've been Sophie's foster mother for six months. In all that time, she's never gotten excited about anything, but this past week she's been ticking off the seconds until she could come here. Every prospective adoptive couple has signed off on her quickly. I'll check on a few things this week, and when you're in the office on Wednesday, we'll go over options. She needs a family, or she's going to age out of the system, with her background we can probably cite those circumstances. Like I said, we'll discuss everything this week and see what we can do."

"Thank you, now, gear up, Scary gets impatient. Sundays are pretty much his one decompress day a week, and he loves a long ride."

"I also think he's impatient to take his future step-daughter for a ride." Megan motioned to where Scary adjusted Sophie's helmet and talked to her softly, probably giving her a quick lesson.

"Don't get my hopes up."

"I'll work it out. This is precisely the family for her and I'll do everything within my power to make sure she gets it."

He just nodded because he couldn't get words passed the lump in his throat. Two men he loved, possibly a daughter in the near future. A year ago, his life was empty except for Brody and Mina, now he had too much, and it still overwhelmed him.

He walked toward Tank and Scary who crouched on either side of Sophie—soon-to-be Juvie. His men looked his way and smiled, but what made it even better was the smile on Sophie's face—it was subtle, but there and that meant almost everything to him right then. This right here couldn't get much better.

15 WOULD ELIJAH LIKE HIS PLACE

He smoothed back his long hair and checked himself in the mirror, this would be the first real date with just him and Elijah. The black button up dress shirt was the nicest he had besides the suit he'd bought for their first date in Atlanta. He'd rolled the sleeves up over his tattooed forearms, and the top two buttons were undone exposing the thick hair on his chest. Jeans and boots completed it, and it was the best it was going to get. His face was all hard angles, lines beside his eyes and the scars.

Scary always turned into his buffer, but there wouldn't be that safety zone tonight. The date was all on him, and again, he didn't know if he could keep Elijah's interest. He hated being that insecure, before Elijah it hadn't fucking mattered. Years had passed since he'd spent so much time looking in a mirror.

He turned away and walked out of his private bathroom. He checked over his bedroom but knew it was as spotless as the rest of the house. He'd grown up in a shithole, so he took a lot of pride in his home. The cabin was way back in the woods with a lake behind it. He'd bought the land not long after he'd move there and spent almost a year living in a one bedroom, small trailer with barely enough room for him to move around. He'd built his place with his own hands, and he wanted to share that with Elijah.

He'd gone into work the day shift at Brawlers, and Scary would work the night one for him so he'd have a private date with Elijah. They'd talked about it the other night. Yes, they were sharing the man, but it was important to them to have alone time with Elijah. They'd also talked about what would happen when they asked him to move in with them and if Sophie became a part of their family as they hoped. It would be easier to live in town to be closer to school, but they'd keep Tank's cabin for private time and family getaways.

Shaking his head, he smiled as he thought about family. He was forty-three, he'd never thought about a partner, much less kids, but that's what was on his mind. All that would work itself out later, tonight it was about him and Elijah. He checked his watch and noticed Elijah would be there any minute.

The closer he drew to the kitchen the scents of dinner filled the rooms. He wasn't much of a cook, but there were a few things he could make well, and lasagna was one of them. His kitchen was modern, stainless steel and belied his lack of cooking skills. The rest of the house was rustic and comfortable. He'd started a fire and set the table. Everything was ready—he hoped.

The sound of tires on gravel had him hurrying for the front door. He opened it and stepped out onto the wraparound porch. He had more house than he needed but he loved it.

He felt his lips pull into a broad smile as Elijah got out of his car and waved, and he descended the steps to meet his man halfway. Elijah was dressed similarly to him, jeans and dress shoes instead of boots, his button up shirt was pale blue—a color he seemed to favor.

"This is gorgeous." Awe filled Elijah's voice, and he loved that Elijah liked his home.

Elijah lifted onto his toes and kissed him, a part of him was still taken aback by the action. The smaller man never missed an opportunity to touch him even if it was just a squeeze of his hand or a hug.

Did you find it okay—he asked.

"Your directions were great, doesn't hurt there's only one marked drive for the last ten miles."

Sorry. I know it is out of the way—he shrugged.

"It's perfect. How did you find this place?"

I built it—he answered.

"By yourself?"

Tank nodded and motioned toward the house. Elijah took his hand and tugged Tank behind him. He loved the man always wanted him close, but it was even. Elijah showed equal attention, and it was like he did it unconsciously.

"Wow, this is, I don't have the words." Elijah released his hands and started to explore.

It did something to him to have Elijah in his space. *Thank you*—he signed when Elijah turned to him. *Do you feel weird with Scary not here*—he had to ask.

"No, I know it's always going to be us, the trio, but I also want time alone with you and Scary. I love having you both around. It just seems natural to want just one of you too. I'm sure we're going to want space from each other—"

He scowled, and Elijah smiled coming to hug his waist.

"Don't even look like that. You and Scary are best friends, but I'm sure you need space from each other sometime."

He nodded.

"And I've been on my own a long time. This having two boyfriends is a bit of an adjustment."

He nodded again because he got it. They were still new and learning about each other, but they wanted Elijah around all the time. If they didn't feel they'd scare him off, they'd make sure they had more time together. But they understood Elijah was independent and used to his space and routine.

"So, what are we doing on our big date?"

Tank started to smirk, and Elijah laughed.

"Aren't you at least gonna feed me first and I don't mean your cock."

His eyes widened, and Elijah snorted.

"I said it before you did."

Okay, you did—he had to admit it was his first thought—*I made dinner. Nothing fancy.*

"Smells like lasagna and if it is, that's my favorite and yes really before you give me that arched brow question."

It still amazed him Elijah could read him so well sometimes he didn't even have to sign. The only other person as attuned with him as Elijah was Scary. They'd had full, silent conversation over the years. Scary could read his facial clues and just know what he was thinking.

Scary is the only one who reads me like you do—He admitted and then led Elijah toward the kitchen, and he set him in one of the chairs. There was already a French Press of fresh coffee on the table and a bottle of water beside his plate. Elijah was obsessed with his coffee.

He served dinner and watched every bite Elijah took, they spoke every now and again, but mostly Elijah kept up a steady stream of conversation. About his new job and Sophie. He was so animated when he talked. The reserved man was coming out his shell becoming comfortable with himself. He hoped some of it had to do with him being happy with Scary and him. That Scary and him made him feel important to them.

He and his best friend were in this, Scary knew from the moment he'd seen Elijah that Elijah was his and it was the same for him. They knew the man was meant to be theirs in every way. Elijah wore his heart on his sleeve and expressive face, Elijah couldn't hide his emotions especially not from them. They'd spent their lives by knowing how to read someone and know within the first few minutes whether they needed to watch their backs. It saved them plenty of times.

Once they finished dinner, Elijah helped him clean up and load the dishwasher. Usually he just hand washed the dishes because it was only him and he regularly ate at the bar or in town.

"I have tomorrow off."

Stay tonight—He'd wanted to ask him all night, but figured he'd have a long ride in the morning to get to work.

"I was going to, but I didn't want to assume. My overnight bag is in the car. Can I ask you something, you don't have to answer—"

He nodded. He had a feeling what it was.

"How did this happen?" Elijah stroked his fingertips gently along his cheek and throat.

So he lifted Elijah onto the counter and moved between his thighs. He told him the whole story, everything about Ian and his old neighborhood. The night he'd gone to tell Ian he was leaving town. Each word he signed caused his body to tense and his heart to pound out of his chest. He hated remembering the first and last time he'd let his guard down.

"I almost lost you," Elijah whispered, and there were tears in his eyes. "Do you know what I thought the first time I saw you?"

He shook his head and moved closer as Elijah rubbed his hands over his chest, toyed with the buttons of his shirt.

"I knew who you were."

He widened his eyes and nodded for him to continue.

"Princess talked about you, and we spent hours working on those videos and flash cards. I don't know why, but she went on and on about you. You sounded—sweet."

He rolled his eyes and Elijah laughed.

"She said you were always by yourself. I assumed she meant you spent a lot of time on the edge. Your scars didn't bother me because I already knew about them. I think I hurt your feelings when I wouldn't look at you that night."

Shrugging his shoulders, he tried to rid Elijah's eyes of the guilt that stole into them.

"I was blushing like crazy. Grown men shouldn't blush when a sexy guy is that close, but there I was, face flaming. And you smelled so good I wanted to put my face against the side of your throat and just take it in." Elijah started to work the buttons of his shirt loose. The younger man leaned forward and placed a kiss in the center of his chest. "And Scary was there too, and I was confused, but I couldn't stop looking at either of you all night."

He let Elijah remove his shirt and then those soft, slender hands were moving over his chest and his stomach, ruffling the thick hair. He was so fucking hard he could come in his jeans at any moment. Never in his life could he remember a lover moaning and shivering just from touching him.

"I always loved hairy men. No manscaping needed and a belly so much better."

Elijah rubbed his cheeks against the hair and kneaded his muscles, Elijah wrapped his lips around one nipple and used his teeth to tug at the barbell. He growled and drove his fingers into Elijah's hair. Jerking Elijah's head back he slammed his lips down on Elijah's, his man opened instantly, and he traced the plump curves of Elijah's mouth. He could kiss Elijah all night. It was something he hadn't had enough of in his life. No one had kissed him until he was twenty-five, plenty had used his body, but fucking was as intimate as anyone wanted to get with him that was until Elijah.

He grunted, and Elijah wrapped his legs around Tank's waist. Slipping his hands under Elijah's ass, he lifted him from the counter and carried him to his bedroom. He laid him on his huge bed and straightened, he kicked off his boots, removed his jeans and underwear, then bent to take off his socks. He stretched to his full height and stood naked, he took his cock in hand and stroked slowly, taking his time. Elijah's gaze fixated on his dick and he licked his lips. He growled as Elijah got up to kneel in the center of the mattress and began removing his shirt.

All that pale, perfect skin exposed for him, flushed pink with arousal. His chest moved with his quick breaths. Elijah laid back and removed the rest of his clothes, he was splayed bare over his bed. Leanly muscled legs parted and what he saw caused him to groan. The base of a plug was exposed.

"I wanted to be—"

Embarrassment clearly stole whatever else Elijah was going to say. He strode to his nightstand and pulled out the new box of condoms, tore it open and quickly sheathed his aching dick. The lube lay on the edge of the mattress. His control was at a minimum when it came to Elijah, but he wanted tonight to be different. His chest was rising and falling quickly with his labored breaths, every inch of him was primed and ready. He hated not being in control, but the man in front of him stole it so quickly. The air in the room felt cold against his overheated body. His thighs flexed as he jerked his cock a few more times.

He moved to sit cross-legged on the bed and patted his thighs as Elijah rolled to his knees. His lover knee walked until he settled onto his lap and Elijah wrapped his long legs around him. He'd dreamed of that moment. Reaching behind Elijah, he took the base of the plug and tugged, shallow thrusting it into Elijah's hole.

"Tank, feels s'good, you feel," Elijah whimpered, and pre-come wet his belly as Elijah's slim cock jerked where it was trapped between them. "Better."

He gently removed the plug and set it aside, he brought his fingertips back and tested Elijah's stretched entrance. He didn't waste time, he lubed his dick and pressed the head to Elijah. The man didn't need prodding because he lifted and started lowering onto his cock. The squeeze was out of the fucking world. Even stretched the man was too tight.

He was finally balls deep in Elijah, and they both breathed heavily. Elijah's gaze met his and held, he curved his hands around the man's perfect plump ass. He started a slow, agonizing rhythm, drawing out their shared pleasure. Elijah's short nails dug into the muscles of his back, their lips brushed with every lift and fall, and through it all, they never broke eye contact.

It was intimate and overwhelming. Elijah moaned and shook, rolling his hips. The buildup was slow, but the intensity was almost more than he could take and then they were both groaning as they kissed. He pulled Elijah's cheeks apart, massaged the stretched skin that massaged his cock. Elijah's hand was working a furious pace between them, and then hot seed coated the hair on his belly. Elijah's hips arched and the contractions of Elijah's hole was all he needed to empty everything into the latex.

"Tank, I—"

He looked at Elijah to find tears slowly sliding down his cheeks. He embraced Elijah and held him tightly to his chest as he buried his face in the crook of Elijah's neck, inhaling the tang of sweat and sex. He never wanted to be parted from Elijah. He knew no matter what happened he would do anything to make Elijah and their family happy.

16 HELL RIDES INTO TOWN

Scary glared at Elijah as the man carried on a secret conversation with Twitch. His newest bartender was small and femme, useless in a brawl, but the man kept bringing the men in so he didn't fucking complain much. Although his man getting friendly with Twitch, he didn't know if he liked that shit. He walked up behind Elijah and bracketed Elijah's body with his arms. The move had the two grinning men separating quickly.

"What are you two plotting?"

"Why would we be plotting anything? I like your man, he's nice." Twitch's voice was low and sweet.

For all of Twitch's flamboyant attitude he'd noticed Twitch spent a lot of time alone on his breaks, he even avoided the flirting and the offers of hookups. Twitch just celebrated his twenty-second birthday. At that age—fuck, he'd reached the when I was your age status. He was officially old.

"He's mine, stop trying to get in his pants."

Twitch's face went ashen, and he backed up until he hit the counter under the register. He needed to get one of the crew to toughen him up.

"You're scaring him, stop scowling." Elijah spun on the stool and wrapped his arms around his neck.

Elijah kissed the scowl in question.

"You fucking love it, quit pretending otherwise. The second you saw me you wanted me."

"I never said I didn't."

"Office," Scary ordered.

A rough chuckle drew his attention, and he turned to find Tank shaking his head. He moved to the side to give Tank access to Elijah. Tank stepped forward and leaned down, without hesitation Elijah tilted his chin.

He glanced around and found no one paying attention, Elijah was becoming as much of a figure around there as them and the crew. With Elijah's new schedule he was working in Atlanta, they didn't get to see each other nearly as much as they liked. Overnights were unheard of, but Elijah promised once he worked everything out they'd spend more time. A compromise was nights at Brawlers. Shit was still new, so they had some kinks to work out. Didn't mean he had to fucking like it. He still hadn't got his one-on-one date with his man.

The door opened, and an unfamiliar group walked in. First glance Scary knew trouble just entered. Their regulars knew if they started shit while Elijah was on the premises they wouldn't find their fucking bodies. One, in particular, caught his attention. Shaved head, caramel skin and mustache with a long goatee, the rage burning in the man's eyes was what put Scary on edge. He knew that look well. The man was as tall as him but broader.

He slapped Tank's back, and when his friend looked up, he nodded toward the door. Instantly they placed themselves between Elijah and the room. Nothing was more important than the man behind them. Crave could spot a potential bloodbath so why the fuck he let this group in he'd find out later.

Studying the rest of the group, another one caught his attention, and he knew when Tank realized it because he stiffened beside him. He darted a look at Tank to find his fists clenching and relaxing, the coldness he hadn't seen in months replaced the warmth of minutes before. Hell had just ridden into town—Ian Jones. What the fuck was that closeted fucker doing there?

Scary reached back to tap Elijah's thigh and motioned to Tank. He knew the minute Elijah touched Tank some of the rage faded, but not all of it. Elijah was talking to Tank in a low, soothing tone, he couldn't make it out, although he didn't think the words mattered. It was the love he sensed in them. Their man loved them, and that meant he had to keep himself and Tank out of jail.

"Nice place you got here, Brawler."

He sneered at his old name. "Nicer before your fucking ass walked through the door. A reason you here," Scary asked.

Scary didn't like the look the man was giving Tank. It was a mixture of lust and rage, tinged with a bit of insanity. Ian was always a crazy son of a bitch and believed laws were always flexible. Ian was just stupid enough to think he could pick back up where he and Tank left off before Ian tried to kill him.

"We're headed to the East Coast, heard about your little bar."

The condescending tone couldn't be mistaken for anything other than disgust. Apparently, Ian was still hiding in that closet.

"Thought I'd stop in and see some old friends. Tank, still breathing I see."

Tank started to lunge forward until Scary noticed the arms around his waist.

"Twitch, get Scary and Tank a pint please and a shot." Elijah's voice rose above the conversation and music.

"Refill on your coffee, Elijah?"

"Thanks, Twitch."

Fingers hooked in his jean loop, and he felt the tiny nudge, nothing obvious, he was sure Elijah did the same to Tank. As if in silent agreement they stepped aside, but Elijah didn't step up to move between them. He stayed where if something went down they could easy shield him again. Elijah instinctively knew what they needed without ever asking or being told.

Ian's gaze fell on Elijah, and the blatant lust in that look made him want to rip the fucker's throat out.

"Doesn't seem your place would bring in the high-class ass, how much?"

"Excuse me?" Elijah's voice went from friendly to pissed.

"Bend you over, never know the ass I'm plowing—"

"You can stop right there. I'm sure you've as you so eloquently put it plowed plenty of ass knowing it was male. Now, if you want to have a drink with the rest of your friends you're more than welcome, this is a public place, but don't piss off my men."

Elijah resumed his seat on the stool, and Scary almost chuckled at the bored look on his cute face. He watched as Bull, another of his bouncers, stepped up to his right.

A few quick, discreet hand gestures and he knew Bull had Elijah if Ian and his crew decided to get froggy.

"Bitch, do you know—"

"Oh, I can safely assume you're Ian." Ian's name came out like a curse.

He'd paddle Elijah's ass later, but he was proud his man was standing his ground. He'd only heard Elijah's voice go that cold and clipped the night they went to the country club.

"Telling your boyfriend about me, Tank?"

He noticed Tank's snarl and heard the low rumble of a growl. He knew the only reason his best friend hadn't flattened the bastard yet was that Elijah was in the line of fire. He watched as Elijah tapped Tank's arm and Tank turned to look down at Elijah.

Hi, baby—Elijah signed.

Hey—Tank's entire focus turned on Elijah.

Come here—Elijah's lips pulled into a sexy grin, and he gripped the front of Tank's shirt and gave a tug. *Missed you today*—Elijah bit his bottom lip.

A small smile tilted the harsh lines of Tank's mouth. Elijah was a fucking genius with a death wish. Scary turned away from Tank and Elijah to let them have their moment. The rage in Ian's eyes amused him.

The other four men behind Ian sneered, but he could tell they were uncomfortable watching two men close to making out at the bar. His crew could take care of them, but the silent one who hadn't said a word or made a move stared off into space, but every line of his body screamed he was ready for battle at any minute.

"Do you gotta fucking do—"

"This is our bar, Elijah and Tank can do what the fuck they want."

A strange sense of satisfaction came over him at the widening of Ian's eyes when Scary felt soft fingertips stroke along his tattooed forearm. He looked at Elijah and loved the fucking smile widening his bite-worthy lips.

"Yeah, baby, ours, don't get too cocky about it, you're a silent partner. No high tea or symphonies." He snorted, actually fucking snorted when Elijah flipped him off. They'd completely corrupted their boy. "You're asking for punishment."

Elijah rolled his eyes and focused his attention back on Tank.

"Now, have a fucking seat, drink a bit as Elijah suggested, but you make one wrong fucking move, and my crew will take y'all out. You're on our turf, and you'll play by our damn rules."

Ian turned and headed for the door, his crew tight on his heels. He knew it was too easy and they hadn't seen the last of Ian. He just wondered how much trouble that fucker would cause before they got him out of town. That's when he noticed the huge man hadn't left, he stood there staring at Tank and Elijah. Some war raged in the dead-eyed gaze.

He growled loud enough to get the man's attention. The stranger grunted and strode toward the door. The crowd separated in his wake. He didn't turn back to Elijah and Tank until he saw them gone.

"Something we have to keep an eye on, boss?" Bull asked.

"Yeah, let Crave and the rest know. We might have a battle on our hands."

"Got it." The older man walked toward the front exit.

He assumed Bull was going to talk to Crave to pass on the info. He reached out and slapped Tank's back.

"You okay, man?"

Tank nodded, but he knew it was a fucking lie. The fucker tried to kill Tank to save his ass, nothing about that was okay.

Someone needs to have Elijah six—Tank's hands moved with fervor.

"We'll take care of it and don't you argue." He pointed at Elijah.

"I do have a modicum of intelligence, and that man doesn't like me very much."

"You weren't helping the cause getting all—"

"I'm not hiding affection for Tank. I wouldn't do that to either of you."

"We know, but Ian—"

"He tried to kill Tank." Elijah's hands absently stroked Tank's chest as if to reassure himself that Tank was still there.

It still amazed him how much Elijah cared—loved them. Even if he hadn't said the words, they both knew how Elijah felt.

"You won't have to worry about me for a few days though. I'm staying in Atlanta. I'm spending time with Juvie. Kam and I have some paperwork to fill out to petition for adoption. I also need to have a meeting with her caseworker."

"You sure about this?"

That earned him another eye roll.

"You knew I was already thinking about it. You told me I was chicken shit because I wouldn't admit it. Is this going to be—"

"Shut up, Juvie wouldn't survive with anyone but us."

She is not that bad—Tank was already the little shit's champion.

He could already see Tank and Elijah spoiling the future Crime Boss. It was going to be up to him to keep their perspective daughter out of prison.

"She is. Let's go home and spend some fucking time together before our man abandons us again."

"Don't pout, it's not attractive on a terrifying man your size."

"You love my size."

"Never said I didn't."

"I'll grab our packs and helmets then I'll be back."

Scary left Tank and Elijah wrapped around each other. His mind jumped from the clusterfuck that was Ian's reappearance and spending time with Elijah. He didn't like the time apart. At least when Elijah was mayor they could see him every day, but now—he wouldn't be a bastard, this was Elijah's dream job. One more bonus was they could take care of Ian and figure out his plan before Elijah came home. Why couldn't shit just be simple and finally go their way? Hadn't they fucking paid enough penance for past sins? Apparently fucking not. He collected his and Tank's things so he could hurry back to Elijah, then they could get their man home.

17 A WEEKEND WITH JUVIE

The trip to Atlanta seemed to speed by, but the one home dragged out forever. Elijah was exhausted. It turned into endless meetings with his lawyer, Juvie's caseworker who seemed shocked someone wanted to adopt her and everything else which needed to be done for his job. He'd signed up for the *IMPACT* training and scheduled an evaluation. Hopefully, the process would shorten since he'd already picked Juvie. He was impatient to get her placed with him so he could have his lawyer petition for adoption.

He and Kam talked at length about whether to tell Juvie or not. It was also her choice whether she wanted to join his family or not, to be honest, it was an unconventional one. What if she didn't want to be his daughter—their daughter?

He peeked into the rearview mirror and smiled at Juvie asleep, her head lolled to the side. Kam and Megan wanted to have a date night, and Elijah jumped at the chance to have Juvie spend the weekend. They'd come pick her up on Sunday after everyone got back from their usual run.

It was still early evening, he'd headed out as soon as Juvie got out of school. He could see her excitement about spending time in Powers, but she'd hid it well. He'd also asked about siblings, but they said she was an only child. Over the weekend, they were going to sit down, all four of them and talk about adding her to the family.

Elijah breathed a sigh of relief as he drove passed the Welcome to Powers sign. They were going to stay at Tank's for the weekend. He drove straight through town and headed for Brawlers. Almost three days since he'd seen Scary and Tank, phone calls didn't exactly help. Another half hour and he pulled up to the bar, bikes already lined up in the gravel parking lot. A small group stood nearby, he groaned as he recognized the blond hair. Just great, he stayed in the car and texted Tank he was outside.

Seconds later the front door open and a wall of sexy walked out. Tank and Scary headed his way, already smiling. He loved to see them happy. It was rare before they started dating and it made him happy that he seemed the cause of it.

"Why is our girl being lazy already," Scary asked as he banged on the window.

A grumpy Juvie growled in the backseat, and she raised her hand.

What was he getting himself into with these three?

"Don't even think about it," Elijah warned as he got out.

He got a quick kiss from both of them before Scary opened the back door to let Juvie out. Scary swung her up into his arms until they were eye level.

"Don't be rude," Scary growled right back.

"I didn't say nothing."

"You didn't have to, I could see the snark wheels turning in that little head of yours."

She rubbed her eyes, and for a moment she looked cute all sleepy.

"I see you have a few new regulars."

"Don't get me started." Scary set Juvie on the hood of the car. "Everyone but Ian and the silent one is grumbling about wanting to move on."

"Well, I just wanted to stop by before we headed to Tank's. We'll both be asleep by the time you two get home."

The kitchen is stocked—Tank leaned back against the car and wrapped his muscled arm around Juvie's shoulders making the already tiny girl seem smaller.

He waited for her to try to pull away, but she just put on a bored expression although he almost caught a smile.

She was born premature and had nearly failed to thrive. Juvie would always be small for her age, but the girl had a Napoleon Complex. She was going to be hell on wheels when she hit her teens which were less than a year away. Oh no, he was going to have a teenage daughter, why couldn't he have started with the cute years?

"What, you just got this panicked look on your face?"

"She's going to be a teenager!" It was all he said and apparently, all he needed to say.

"Oh, fuck—do you—"

He hushed Scary as Tank chuckled.

She will be okay—Tank tried to sooth his near mental breakdown.

"You're talking about me," Juvie pouted.

"Have you been practicing?"

"Yes, I brought them with me, but can Tank show me this weekend?" Juvie darted a quick glance at Tank, then down at her hands.

It looked like she was preparing herself for Tank to say no. Tank grunted to get Juvie's attention, and when she looked at him, he placed his hand over his heart.

"He's promising to work on your signs."

"Okay, thanks."

He was about to reach out and lift her eyes to his but caught movement out of the corner of his eye. Suddenly there was a wall of muscle between them and Ian. He stepped up to Juvie and hugged her to his side.

"This is a private conversation," Scary snarled.

"It's okay, we're going home in a minute," he whispered in Juvie's ear. "Why don't you get in and buckle up?"

She only nodded in answer as she hopped off the hood, rushing to the back door. He hated to see her like that—scared.

"I just wanted to say hi to your boy and the little lady."

"Not a fucking chance."

He took in the tense line of Tank's back and shoulders, he stepped up to place his forehead between Tank's shoulder blades. It was taking everything in Tank not to lose himself in years of rage. Scary didn't have the horror of a lover trying to kill him tearing at his control, but Tank did. He wanted to make it all go away and maybe one day he would. Although Tank had a very real reminder every time he caught his reflection in a mirror or window.

"We're heading out," he whispered.

Tank was the first one to turn while Scary watched his back. The big silent man took his face in his calloused hands and leaned down to kiss him.

"Missed sleeping with you two, y'all are both coming to bed when you get home right?"

Tank nodded with his mouth still against his. He took in Tank's features, he'd loved his face since the moment he'd seen him. Lifting his hands, he stroked the tips of his fingers along the scar. A shuddered breath fanned his lips, and he tilted his chin slightly to brush their mouths once more.

He felt the reluctance in Tank to retreat, but he turned around to give Scary his turn.

"Keep the bed warm for us," Scary whispered seconds before he took his mouth in a rough kiss.

"Just come home, I'm not getting Juvie up to bail you two out."

"Where the fuck is the love?"

"We'll add in sickness, and in health and midnight bail hearings to our vows."

Scary threw back his head and laughed.

"We'll hold you to it."

"I must be insane."

"Go home, curl up with our girl and relax, we'll wake you when we get home."

"Okay, keep him safe for me," Elijah ordered.

"Definitely. You're kinda scary standing on a bar with a bat."

"That was one time, and it was to keep you two out of jail." He rolled his eyes as he backed away.

"We'll stay right here until you pull out."

He got into his car and looked back at Juvie.

"Is something wrong," she asked in a small voice.

"No, nothing at all. Tank and Scary are just super protective. Want to go see Tank's cabin?"

"The one with the lake?"

"Yes. Tank said he fixed up the guest room for you."

He kept up a steady stream of conversation for the next fifteen minutes it took to get to the turn off for Tank's place. He took the winding road into the woods. Juvie's small gasp from the back seat proved she was impressed with their weekend home.

"What do you think?"

"I've never been in a house that big before. I won't break anything, I promise."

"Tank won't care, accidents happen, but it better not be his TV, he loves his TV, maybe even more than me. You know how men are."

He caught the rolling of her eyes in the rearview, and he pulled to a stop in front of the garage. In minutes he had her, their bags and headed toward the house. He opened the door with the key Tank gave him, it was right next to the key to Scary's house and the one for Brawlers. He quickly stepped inside to deactivate the alarm.

Juvie was turning in circles taking in the huge great room and the open kitchen. Floor to ceiling glass showed off the woods and lake behind the cabin. She seemed sufficiently impressed.

"Come on, I'll show you where you'll be sleeping." He pointed toward the hallway, and she skipped ahead of him. "Third door," he called out as she skidded to a halt and her mouth fell open.

"The bed is huge, I'm gonna need a ladder."

"Scary sleeps here, so the bed has to be that big." He watched her chew on her bottom lip. "What? You can ask me anything, talk to me about whatever you want."

"Do you love them?"

"Yes, I do, but I haven't told them, so shush, our secret for now."

"Why do you—"

"Sit down with me for a minute." He led her to the bed and helped her up, then he climbed up to sit beside her. The bed was too big for ordinary people.

"I'm going to tell you a story. My brother Brody found this great guy. I was a little skeptical about him dating Trouble, but then I met Trouble's friends, and they were like this amazing little family. I was jealous."

"Why?"

"I raised Brody. When our parents died, they left me in charge of him. It was the two of us against the world, and suddenly I was on the outside."

"You didn't belong. I don't—"

"You belong, don't think otherwise." He gave her a quick hug. "Now, when I met the friends there was this huge, grumpy bear. All growl and mean looks, but I liked him, instantly felt safe. It just wasn't supposed to be. Then almost a year later I meet another guy. He was sweet, maybe a little scary looking and again I felt safe. Security is a big thing when you don't have it for a long time or even ever. Do you understand that?" He asked the question even knowing the answer.

"Yeah."

"Well, I fell in love with both of them. It's not right for everyone, but it is for me. Well, not at first, it was weird. It doesn't change how I feel though. Do you find it uncomfortable that I have two partners?"

"No, but—"

"But what?"

"You won't be mad if I tell you something."

"Of course, I won't be mad."

"I like this girl at school."

Oh man, girl problems, he so wasn't equipped for this. "And? Have you talked to Kam or Megan?"

She shook her head.

Why did she think he'd be mad if she told him she was lesbian? Kam and Megan were her foster parents, well, Kam, was, everyone in his family was gay or bisexual or allies. Maybe she just didn't understand all of it yet. He was extremely flattered she talked to him first.

"When did you know you liked—" She paused and looked down at her hands.

"When did I know I was gay?" She nodded. "A part of me thinks I always knew, but I had my first crush on a boy when I was your age. Does this girl know?"

"Everyone thinks I'm weird and they don't talk to me."

"Well, they don't know what they're missing. Beneath all the attitude and snark I think you're great. Okay, not true, I like the attitude and snark too. You've met the family."

She laughed, a real one and a smile lit up her beautiful, heart-shaped face.

"I never claimed to be normal, I just look that way. Want to have some dinner and talk about this girl you like? It's been awhile since I talked about girl problems. Brody only dated one girl through high school, but I've been through him having crushes on boys and girls since he was ten."

They got through making dinner without burning down the house. He was an okay cook, but not the best. He'd lived on takeout and restaurant food for the last decade if he wasn't eating at Brody's or with the guys. There were more laughs and smiles, they watched some action movie and Juvie apparently loved explosions and fight scenes. He saw a lot of action movies in his future, maybe he could pass that off to Scary or Tank.

He was already planning ahead with the four of them. All he knew, even if he was jumping the gun, he already knew what he wanted. Her head fell to his shoulder, and he looked down to find her almost asleep.

"Off to bed with you."

"Can I stay up and wait for Tank and Scary."

"No, they won't be home until probably three or four depending on paperwork."

"Fine." She pouted and got to her feet.

"Are you too old and wise to be tucked in?"

"Yes, but I'll let you do it this once."

"Yes!" He fist-pumped and jumped off the couch. "Can I read you a bedtime story?" He hit the power button on the remote and followed her.

She rolled her eyes as at him and took off mumbling to herself.

Oh, the life of an embarrassing parent, he was looking forward to it. He walked into the bedroom just as she crawled under the covers. He leaned over and looked at her.

"I'm ecstatic you came to visit this weekend."

"I wish I could stay here all the time."

"We'll see what we can do about you spending more time with us okay?"

She nodded, and he tucked the covers under her chin.

"Get some sleep, and we'll pick some stuff to do tomorrow morning while Scary and Tank sleep. They took off tomorrow night so we could all do something." They also had a huge surprise for her the next afternoon. He'd talked it over with Kam, and she'd agreed without question.

"Thanks for you know—"

He nodded and leaned forward to kiss her forehead. "Good night, Juvie, if you need anything in the night I showed you where we'd be." He straightened as she rolled away from him covering her head with the covers.

Reluctantly he stepped away from the bed and headed for the bedroom to shower, then get some sleep. He wanted a few minutes with his men before they had to get some rest. They tended to put off sleep to spend time with him, and he hated for them to go to work exhausted, it didn't help them stay on guard at Brawlers.

Anything happening to them wasn't an option. He didn't know what he'd do if he lost one or both of them. Elijah pushed away the depressing direction of his thoughts were, grabbed pajama bottoms and headed to take a shower. They'd be home before he knew it.

18 HE IS CRAZY ENOUGH TO THINK HE GETS A SECOND CHANCE

They'd reached capacity an hour before, and he'd left Crave to man the door. He didn't like Ian being in his damn bar, but he wanted to be the bigger man. Ian had no power over him. That shit ended two decades ago. Why the fuck is Ian back was still a mystery? Ian looked nearly the same, except his blond hair was streaked with silver, and he had deep lines beside his eyes. At one time, he could've seen himself falling for Ian, but that ended before the man ever took a knife to his throat.

"Another pint, Tank?" Twitch's sweet voice pulled him from his thoughts.

The pretty man didn't exactly fit with the rest of the Brawler Crew, but they did one hell of a job when they hired him. The man proved useless in a physical fight, although Twitch had a way with talking the mean drunks down.

He shook his head. Twitch knew most of the basic signs and letters yet not enough to carry on a full conversation.

What he wanted was to go home to Elijah and Juvie, he knew both were probably asleep, but he could curl up with his man. Unfortunately, a crowd that size it required all hands.

Scanning said crowd, he was thankful everyone seemed more intent on drinking and finding a fuck for the night than fighting. Ian and his crew were in the far corner booth except for the quiet one who'd taken a place at the other end of the bar with his back to the wall. The man's body language broadcasted he was always ready for a fight. His fists clenched and his eyes constantly searched the room. He didn't sense trouble though. For a minute, he pondered why the guy rode with Ian. He'd bet his half of the bar the guy was gay. The stranger's eyes stopped here and there on certain men—ones that looked exactly like him.

"Your sixth sense zeroing in on trouble?" Scary appeared on his right and leaned forward to rest his forearms on the bar.

Calm before the storm—he signed quickly. He was damn good at his job.

They wouldn't have kept their place in one piece if he didn't maintain the peace. Yeah, the law loved to give them shit, but with a bar like theirs, it drew a lot of attention.

"Ian needs to move his ass on out of town."

He nodded in agreement. They were both on the same page with that one.

"Ya wanna head out early and curl up with Elijah?"

You need me here—He'd jump at the chance to spend a night sleeping with their man. Elijah spent three days away. The time apart was getting to be too much to handle. He knew the situation wasn't permanent, but it didn't make it any less frustrating.

"Man, go home, a few more hours until last call then I'll be home myself."

He gave Scary a look that asked was he sure.

"I'm sure, get out."

Thank you—He didn't wait as he spun and headed for the office to grab his pack and helmet. Twenty minutes he could be home, jump in the shower and hold Elijah until Scary came in.

He walked into the office and didn't bother closing the door behind him. He didn't grab his laptop, he'd do tonight and tomorrow's accounting adding it to Monday's paperwork.

Tank sensed someone entering the room, and he spun in time to see Ian stopped just inside. He opened his mouth to tell the fucker to get out, but then he remembered.

"Finally got you alone, did you—"

He growled, and the bastard had the nerve to smile. Ian advanced—his mouth pushing brutally to his. Rage and guilt exploded in his chest, and he placed his hands on Ian's chest and pushed.

Ian recovered and kept coming. "You remember how I like it rough. A good fight leads to better fucking. I missed that tight—"

The fucker didn't have a chance to finish because he swung and connected hard with his jaw. He hadn't regretted his silence much over the years except with Elijah and right then.

Ian fell as the door flew open and banged against the wall. Scary stood framed in the doorway, a question in

Scary's gaze and he nodded to let his best friend know he was okay.

"I think you've worn out your welcome, Ian, get your ass and crew, get the fuck out of our bar. Tank, ya wanna take out the trash?"

He nodded as he bent down and grabbed Ian by the scruff of his shirt, jerked him to his feet and tiptoed his ass to the front door. A few signals and Bull headed toward Ian's crew. Ian was calling him every name in the book and throwing out threats he'd never be able to back up. Crave opened the door, slightly bowing as he motioned toward the open door with a flourish with an impish grin on his face. That should have looked weird on a man of his bulk, but it was so Crave.

With one hard push, he sent Ian stumbling out the door. His crew wasn't far behind him. A few slurs and even more threats, the last member of the crew walked out without a word. A weight seemed to lift having rid his turf of those bastards.

"You okay, man," Scary asked.

He turned to find Scary with an actual concerned expression. They'd known each other decades, and he'd never seen that before. It was odd, and he didn't know what to make of it.

The only answer he gave was a nod.

"Let's get your shit and send you home."

Will Elijah—a growl stopped him, and he dropped his hands.

"Elijah won't think shit and don't start getting stupid on me. But I know you, and you'll feel better after you tell him. That was Ian's bullshit, had nothing to do with you."

He swallowed hard, he did feel guilty, and he didn't understand why. Ian was insane if he thought that shit was going to work, he had Elijah and a chance for a real family. The three of them, and hopefully Sophie. He wouldn't screw it up for anything.

Scary watched his back and stayed close the whole time until he was on his way toward home.

✦ ✦ ✦

Fifteen minutes later he rode along his curving drive and hit the button for his garage. He drove inside, turned off his bike and kicked the stand down. Playing the last part of the night through his head wasn't getting him anywhere. Ian trying to pick up where they left off, Scary's odd behavior and it was screwing his head up.

He lowered the garage door, exited through the side door and strode toward the house. It was only a little after midnight, but his house was dark. He made his way inside and reset the alarm before heading for his bedroom, but stopped at the room he knew Sophie was sleeping. Nudging the door open, he peeked inside and only found a tiny mound curled up dead center of the bed. Walking softly into the room, he eased toward the bed and lifted the covers, he heard soft little snores and figured she was okay under there.

Lowering the blanket, he left the room and headed for his. The door stood open, and a dim light from the bathroom door illuminated the bed. Elijah was curled on his side, a pillow behind him and another wrapped in his arms. He smiled as he headed for the bathroom to shower off Brawlers, Bull loved his cigars, but Elijah hated the smell.

A quick scrub and a search for sleep pants, he preferred to sleep naked, but if Sophie needed them in the night, he'd suffer through wearing pajama bottoms. He approached the bed, removed the pillow from behind Elijah and took its place.

"Tank—" Elijah sleepily sighed as he snuggled back into his body. "You're home early, you okay?"

He tapped Elijah's hip, and the man didn't hesitate to turn toward him.

Ian followed me to the office and kissed me—he signed without hesitation wanting to get it out.

"Are you okay, I hope you knocked him on his ass."

He nodded.

"Good, you're mine, and I'm not all that great at sharing."

Soft lips conformed to his—the action slow and gentle. It still amazed him a man like Elijah would treat him with tenderness. It shouldn't though because it was Elijah's way he showed people he cared. Elijah's slender arms curled around his neck.

"Scary staying until last call, he isn't doing the paperwork, is he?"

He snorted at the horror in Elijah's voice. Elijah had to deal with a call from the accountant after their solo date, and Scary handled the deposit and receipts. He shook his head.

"Oh good, I don't think Bruno has any hair left to pull out."

He sighed and buried his face in the crook of Elijah's shoulder.

"You felt all guilty, didn't you?"

Another nod, because he couldn't deny it. He didn't want another man in his bed, well, there was Scary, but they both like sleeping beside Elijah. It was the best sleep they'd gotten in years.

"I know you wouldn't cheat, like I know Scary wouldn't. I trust both of you without question, but I also know you own a bar, sexy men everywhere. Who could resist trying to get my sexy men in bed?" Hands caught his cheeks and pulled his head back to look at Elijah.

Crazy—he gruffly laughed.

"No, I'm not. I love you both, and you two know it. So, I don't want to hear your bullshit—"

His eyes went wide at the I love you, but even wider at Elijah cussing.

"I wanted to tell you both at the same time, didn't quite happen. My brain's still asleep."

He cuddled Elijah close to his chest.

"Okay, we'll sleep until Scary gets home."

Elijah's warm breath fanned his chest as he spoke. He'd never thought he'd be much of a cuddler, but it was just natural with Elijah. There was no way he could resist holding his man close. He listened to Elijah's breaths evening out, and the man relaxed completely in his arms. He'd worried for nothing. He should have known Elijah trusted him. Elijah wouldn't have agreed to be theirs if he didn't. That took a lot of faith, something he hadn't thought he possessed until Elijah came into his life.

He let his eyes close, but doubted he'd sleep, it was a still a little early for him. He'd watch over Elijah until Scary came in, then they'd have a little alone time with Elijah before they slept while Elijah spent the morning with Sophie.

19 A DAY WITH THE FAMILY AND OTHER SURREAL SHIT

Sitting back on the bank of the lake, Scary bent his legs and rested his forearms on his knees as he watched Tank, Elijah and Juvie walking along the shore. Things were fucked up in his head. It was like a sledgehammer to the gut. His gaze lingered on Elijah, then Tank. The man was his best friend, and they'd gone through hell together over the years. They always had each other's backs no matter what.

This was different, a disturbing and surreal different. It wasn't as if he hadn't noticed his best friend over the years. Maybe back when he first realized he was gay, he'd had a thing for Tank. What he thought about now wasn't about some teenage crush. He could keep it to his damn self, never act on it, but it would be—dammit, he scrubbed his hands over his face.

He didn't need any more complications in his life. The only natural thing he had was their relationship with

Elijah. He removed his face from his hands as he sensed someone sitting down beside him.

"Are you mad," Juvie asked.

The tone of her voice became all too familiar. She used it when she felt insecure.

"Naw, just thinking."

"Sorry I got you up early."

"No big deal, I've gone days on less sleep. We don't exactly get to spend much time with Elijah lately."

"Because he's been visiting me?"

"Whatever bullshit is going on in your head, knock it off." He slung an arm around her and pulled her into his side. "We're good, okay?"

She only nodded.

"Elijah's still getting used to his new job. He does days, and we do nights, we'll work it out." He made it sound so fucking easy, but it wasn't.

"Okay."

They fell into silence as they looked out over the lake. He glanced out the corner of his eye as he watched Tank and Elijah together. A sharp slash of envy sent a painful slice through his chest. His head was all fucked up.

Waking up earlier, he'd found himself face to face with Tank with their chests pressed together and his hand on Tank's hip. The man's mouth close to his and for a second he'd almost leaned in. He'd rolled from the bed as quick as possible before he'd done something stupid—something he couldn't take back.

"Come on, kid, let's get moving. Tank, Elijah, we gotta go," he hollered as he pushed Juvie and himself to their feet.

Elijah and Tank looked so happy as they closed the distance and he felt like such a bastard. He drew Elijah into his arms and kissed him. He almost reached out to bring Tank closer, but Tank walked off with Juvie.

"You okay?" Elijah leaned back to look up at him with a concerned expression.

"Yeah, I'm good. I just know Trouble has an appointment and I don't want her surprise to wait."

"She's going to be so excited."

"You're almost as damn excited as she is."

"I know right." Elijah practically bounced. "I barely kept from telling her."

"Well, let's get our asses moving."

"Yes, sir." Elijah mock-saluted and took off after Tank and Juvie.

He jogged to catch up. Juvie was already on the seat behind Tank. Elijah adjusted her chin strap and Juvie muttered it was fine. He walked over to his bike to wait for Elijah. Maybe the ride into town would clear his head, or he needed some time alone, some distance between the three of them.

He grimaced at the thought, he couldn't do that because it would hurt Elijah. They'd made a pact there'd be no secrets between them, but this wasn't something he could share. What would Elijah and Tank think? He couldn't fuck with a lifelong friendship or the dynamic they'd comfortably settled into. He could get over it; he didn't have a choice.

It wasn't long before they pulled out and headed to town. He hoped Juvie liked her surprise. They hadn't discussed it, but they'd noticed she was a little jealous of Princess' pierced ears—her hair. They wanted her to feel part of the crew. The adoption wasn't a sure thing, but they wanted her to know she'd always be one of them. Children and adults needed to know they belonged somewhere.

After getting her ears pierced the four of them would go to dinner to discuss becoming a part of their family and crew. He pulled up in front of the shop and backed up to the curb, Tank followed.

"Look at our bad ass mini-biker in training." Lucky came barreling out the door.

"Lucky," Juvie called out.

Tank reached back to help her off the bike and didn't let go of her hand until she had her feet safely on the ground. She headed instantly for the shop, and Lucky opened the door. Juvie ducked under his arm and disappeared inside.

"Don't ruin the surprise," Elijah ordered as he swung off and took off after Lucky and Juvie.

Tank grunted to get his attention, he turned his head to find Tank standing close—too close.

What is wrong with you—Tank's large hands moved in a sharp, agitated rhythm.

"Nothing, man, just fucking tired." He dismounted and started to head for the shop when Tank barred his way. He didn't want to fucking do this right now.

Bullshit—Tank reached for him.

He didn't stop himself in time and stepped back. Tank's eyes widened then narrowed, the muscles in his jaw ticking as Tank clenched his jaw.

Never—He grabbed Tanks hands and stopped him, released them quickly to take another step back.

"Don't try that shit with me. You start issuing fucking orders, and you know where it'll end up."

Scary, what did I do—Tank asked and let his arms fall to his sides.

"Nothing, it's fine. Let's get inside, or we'll miss Juvie getting her ears pierced."

Tank nodded, but the sadness in his best friend's eyes fucking killed him. He didn't want to push his best friend away, but he couldn't handle dealing with his feelings yet. Especially when Scary shouldn't be having them at all. He motioned for Tank to go ahead of him. He needed to get his shit straight before he walked into the shop. Landon could read someone faster than anything.

He jogged a few steps to catch the door Tank held open. His front collided with Tank's back. The pace of his heart sped up, and his hand rested on Tank's side. Tank walked ahead as if nothing happened, nothing had for Tank, but he was close to losing his mind. If he hadn't already lost it.

♦ ♦ ♦

A few hours later they set in a booth at the back of the diner. Juvie looked over the menu. The girl didn't know what to choose. He nudged Elijah, and his man cleared his throat.

"Juvie, we wanted to talk to you." Elijah's voice sounded soft and hesitant.

He knew Elijah was nervous Juvie would say she didn't want to be adopted or be a part of their family. He also knew Elijah wasn't happy they had to keep their relationship secret until after the placement came through. A triad couple wouldn't be acceptable.

"Um, about what," Juvie asked as she set her menu aside and lowered her hands to her lap.

"It's nothing bad, we just wanted to ask you something. Do you like spending time with us?"

"Yes, it's nice."

"Would you like if I petitioned to adopt you?"

"Really?" Her voice rose several octaves, and her almond shaped eyes widened.

"Yes, Kam and I've talked about it. I've also met with your caseworker. There's still a lot that I need to do, and I can't tell you for sure it'll happen. I know that isn't what you want to hear, but I wanted you to at least have a choice if I continue with it or not."

"Y'all want me to live with y'all?" She looked around at all three of them.

Tank nodded and wrapped his arm around her. Elijah just smiled and reached across the table to take her hand.

He looked around at the people he considered family. Even if they didn't get to adopt Juvie, he'd make damn sure they stayed in her life. She'd always know she had a place to call home. Something he hadn't had after his mother died until he'd come there.

"Juvie, you'd be living with just me to start out. You know—"

He took Elijah's hand in his when the man's voice broke. "We don't know what will happen if they find out Elijah has two partners."

"So, we have to keep it secret?"

"Just until everything's official. We don't want to ruin our chance of having you come live with us."

He knew they didn't like having to hide their relationship, but they'd discussed it. They could deal with it until Juvie was under Elijah's roof.

"We're not exactly a traditional family," he said.

Juvie rolled her eyes.

"So, what do you think," Elijah asked and held his breath.

"I want to live with y'all."

"Okay, I've got to take some classes, someone will come to my house to check everything out, and I've already submitted to the background checks. When the placement is approved, you'll move in with me, and I'll petition a judge for adoption. Until then though, you'll be able to visit us, and I'll spend time with you when I come down for work."

"Promise," Juvie asked.

He knew she wouldn't take a promise lightly. Kam shared some of Juvie's background. They wouldn't have an easy time of earning her trust. Making her feel secure would always be a challenge.

"Promise," Elijah and him said together.

She turned to look at Tank, and he placed his hand over his heart.

"Now, we're going to have dinner and head home for movies and junk food."

He smiled as she quickly opened her menu.

They still had a lot to do and were up for the challenge. The only thing he had to deal with now was getting his head right and them back to normal. He'd apologize to Tank later. It wasn't Tank and Elijah's fault he was fucking things up. He'd get it right because he wasn't losing his best friend and Elijah. He could deal with a lot of shit, but that wasn't an option.

20 THAT WAS FUCKING SEXY

One last text to Kam to check on Juvie and then he finished getting ready for his date with Scary. Tank offered to cover for Scary since him and Scary hadn't had much time alone recently. He also had to talk with Scary about his concerning behavior. It started to worry them a week ago when Scary distanced himself. He loved the huge man, but the guy was beginning to piss him off.

They were coming up on four months together, and if Scary was having second thoughts, he needed to know. He loved Tank and Scary, but would him and Tank survive as a couple without—he shook his head. The what-ifs weren't going to get him anywhere. Only a long talk and the truth would clear his head of the doubts taking hold.

Scary said to dress casual which wasn't unusual for their time together. He wasn't forced to put on some fancy suit anymore and pretend to be as put together as people expected. He sat on the bench at the end of his bed and put on his dress shoes. His dark jeans and button down shirt would work for wherever they ended up.

The peal of the doorbell had him standing, and he jogged out of his bedroom toward the steps and descended to answer the door. He didn't know why Scary still knocked or rang the bell when he had a key as did Tank.

"Why don't you use your key," he asked as he opened the door.

"It's a date, isn't it all customary and shit to knock?"

"Okay, I'll give you that one. Get in here." He reached out and grabbed Scary's wrist to tug him inside. "You're early."

"I couldn't sit around the house."

He closed the door. Scary stood stiffly. He didn't like the fact the old Scary decided to make a reappearance. The closed off and unhappy one, and he wouldn't let Scary do that to them.

"What the hell is going on with you," he demanded. Tank tried yet failed to get whatever was going on with Scary out of him.

"Don't you start this bullshit too. Tank and I already went a round or two."

"I heard you and Tank spar on a regular basis. That isn't anything new, but you won't talk to either of us. Are you regretting us?"

"No," Scary yelled as he lifted his hands to roughly rub the stubble on his head. "I don't regret us being together."

"Then tell me please." Elijah stepped forward and reached out to grip the sides of Scary's t-shirt. "If you don't want to end things, is Juvie—"

"Hell no, fuck, I love you, and I can't wait for Juvie to come live with us." Scary heavily sighed as he dropped his chin to his chest. "My head if just all fucked up and I don't know—"

"I can't help, and Tank can't help if you won't tell us. You know we're in this together. Equal partnership and no lies."

"What if it's better I fucking keep this one to myself?"

"Not if it's going to make all of us miserable. No matter how much I love you and Tank, I won't come between you two. You've been best friends for decades."

"We're not giving you up. What if I tell you something and it fucks up what we have?"

"Did you cheat on me?"

"Are you fucking kidding me?"

"Well, really that's the worst thing I could come up with."

"It ain't that." Scary retreated until he perched on the back of the couch. "I knew I was gay pretty early. My mom, Monica, always said I needed a good man. She hated I lived in the closet for so long, but—"

"Kinda safer in your neighborhood. Tank's proof of that."

"Yeah, hell, I even kept it from Tank. But I had—"

"Did you love Tank? And not in a best friend way." He felt he already knew the answer.

"I don't know about love, but I noticed him."

"You're still noticing him, aren't you? Did what we have bring it back up?"

Scary dragged his hands up and down his massive thighs and dropped his head back. He watched Scary's Adam's apple bob as he swallowed. Whatever was going on with Scary tore the man apart inside.

"It all hit me. It was like one minute Tank's my best friend, and then we all started—it got so fucking surreal.

Then I fucking saw Ian try to put his hands on Tank and I got, I don't know."

"You got jealous."

"And pissed as fuck."

"So, we've named the problem, what are we going to do about it?"

"Why are you so fucking calm about this? I'm telling you I want to fuck—"

Scary was getting pissed or defensive, it didn't matter which because it ended the same.

"No, you're not telling me you want to sleep with some random man. It's Tank. What changes if you make your intentions known?"

"I lose my best friend and you."

He could take a lot things, but Scary's misery was not one of them. He closed the distance Scary tried to put between them both physically and emotionally. He took Scary's face in his hands and tilted his chin up to lightly brush their lips together. He stroked the strong angles of Scary's handsome features. He adored everything about Scary even his surly nature.

"You're not gonna lose Tank or me, but if you keep pushing us away, you will."

"I don't know if I can take that chance."

"Too damn bad, it's out. You confessed the big bad secret. I didn't run away. I don't think anything is wrong with it. Now, if you wanted to add a fourth..." He playfully growled as he slid his arms to rest over Scary's shoulders, "not happening."

"I've told you before, I've got enough trouble with you."

"But that's when you told me not to think about adopting and see what happened?"

"How do I tell him, baby?"

"You open those sexy lips and tell him the truth. We're going to Brawlers, and we're going to get this shit out of the way. No excuses."

"You're getting a damn foul mouth on you."

"Blame my hot ass boyfriends."

"If this goes south, a bar is probably the best place, I'm gonna need several drinks."

"It'll be fine, and if nothing else, it's out. Tank's scared you regret what we have. He's blaming himself because he thinks he pushed you."

"Let's go."

He followed along quickly as Scary acted like he was on a mission. It wasn't long before they sped toward Brawlers. He held tight to Scary's waist. The man's relaxed posture belied the tension he sensed in Scary. He'd learned to read Scary just as well as Tank, but Scary was the more intense of the two and more adept at hiding his emotions.

There wasn't anything more he wanted in his life than to his family to be happy. If the three of them couldn't work as a unit and be honest with each other, where would that leave them?

Scary slowly rolled to a stop, and then backed into the reserved space beside Tank's bike.

"Maybe we should go home," Scary suggested.

"No, we're gonna solve this here and now. I'm not having both my men miserable because one them is hiding shit."

He dismounted and removed his helmet.

"Get off the bike." He placed his hands on his hips. "Don't make me tell you again."

"You're a bossy little shit, why did I ever think of you as shy?" Scary removed his helmet and swung his leg over the seat.

"I was, then I was corrupted. Quit stalling." He grabbed Scary's wrist and dragged him toward the front door. "Hey, Crave," he greeted the burly blond.

"The pretty boss, you're here as much as your men are."

"And you're the king of exaggeration. Where's my other man?"

"Last I saw, Twitch was giving him shit for being grumpy."

"Let me go save him."

Elijah adored Twitch, but there was a thin line between loving the beautiful man and wanting to wring his neck. Crave opened the door and motioned them inside with a sweep of his arm and a deep bow. Even a mid-week crowd was a bit of a crush. He still held Scary tight as he searched for Tank and found him sitting at the bar.

Surprise showed on Tank's face. He didn't wait for questions just grabbed Tank with his free hand and led them both to the office. Once inside, he released them and locked the door.

"You two need to talk." He walked to the desk and hoisted himself onto it. He motioned to them with a go-ahead motion.

The two stubborn men squared off, assessing each other like opponents in a boxing ring. In the last four months, he'd seen them go at each other. A release of tension, they were all raging testosterone, and he loved them beyond reason. He smiled at his thoughts.

Tank's movements were agitated as he demanded answers and he could barely keep up. He'd watched them have silent arguments plenty of times, but even he couldn't keep up with a pissed off Tank.

"That's not what the fuck this was about and don't try your guilt trip bullshit with me. I never once said you forced me into anything. I wanted Elijah as much as you did."

"Gentlemen, gentleman, please, can you conduct yourselves in a manner that even remotely implies y'all are adults?"

He snickered as he was promptly flipped off by both and then ignored.

"I so feel the love," he playfully whined and pouted.

If Tank and Scary ever did have sex, he wondered if they would survive it. He was jumping ahead a bit. First Scary had to admit what he wanted.

"Fuck this, I'm not arguing with you."

It was the only warning Tank got. It transitioned into slow motion as Tank's back met the door and Scary had Tank's jaw cupped in his hands. Tank seemed frozen, his scarred hands firmly around Scary's wrists. With their slight difference in height, Scary only had to lean down a few inches until his lips hovered over Tank's mouth.

Elijah refused to move so he wouldn't break into the moment. They'd reached the point of no return, and he was nervous—no terrified. He held his breath and waited.

"S'fucking sexy," Scary growled deep in his chest.

Tank's body trembled as his chest moved quickly with his labored breaths. Elijah watched as Tank darted looks from Scary's mouth to his eyes and back again. Scary slammed his mouth onto Tank's and forced Tank harder against the door.

Growls and deep groans filled the small space of the dim office. His own heart kicked up a desperate rhythm as he watched his men clutch at each other. Scary's fingers tangled in the long strands of Tank's hair.

They were sexy together. All inked, hair-roughened skin and thick muscle.

Scary drew back, biting down on Tank's full bottom lip and gently tugged. Elijah took in Tank's flushed cheeks above his beard and his glazed eyes. Tank entirely focused on Scary.

Scary release Tank's lip. "So fucking hard for me."

He bit off a groan as Scary slipped his left hand between his and Tank's bodies. The back of Tank's head banged against wood, and his hips jerked forward. Elijah's hands ached as he realized he had them clenched around the edge of the desk.

"Do you want this," Scary asked in a low, gravelly tone. "When I saw Ian touch you, I could've fucking killed him."

Tank whimpered as he shifted his feet apart.

"No one touches you but me and Elijah, no one."

The possessiveness in Scary's tone dark and primal.

"Do you understand me." It wasn't a question, but a demand.

Tank shakily nodded.

"We're going on a date, the three of us."

Scary and Tank turned to him, they were still pressed closer together. Should he be jealous, something other than turned on? It felt right, it was the three of them like it should be. His two men gravitated toward each other like they did with him.

Elijah didn't realize until right then why they were so close. Scary and Tank may have kept things unconsciously in the friend's only slot to hold tight to their friendship.

Now the truth came out they needed to figure out how to go forward.

He met Tank's gaze and clearly saw the question there. He nodded and smiled sliding off the desk. The distance between him and them was too much, he stepped up to their side and wrapped his arms around them. They each placed a hand on his lower back, and he smiled as he felt their fingers lock together.

The instant rightness he felt as he soaked in their warmth and combined scents brought him the sense of belonging he'd always yearned for, yet hadn't found until them.

21 WHERE THE FUCK WAS ELIJAH

Tank set on the edge of his bed and bent over tying his boots as his brain kept trying to process what happened the night before. He still felt Scary's lips on his for the first time in all the years they'd known each other. Nothing went past the kiss. They'd curled up with Elijah like any other night, but unlike the other nights, Scary's arm laid across Elijah as well as him.

"You're analyzing shit, stop it," Scary ordered as he walked out of the bathroom steam following him with a towel loosely held around his hips.

Apparently, he didn't have to say anything because Scary kept going as he walked toward the bed. "Eyes on me," Scary ordered. Scary stopped in front of him.

His brows rose as he leaned his head back to look up at Scary. He could already see they were going to fight— more than they already did. Fuck, he knew that damn smirk. Scary bent at the waist to push his fists into the mattress beside Tank's thighs. He would not retreat, he would not—dammit, he retreated. Scary chuckled low and dark.

Did Scary only want him because of some momentary jealousy or—

"For a cold bastard, your face is way too expressive."

Scary lifted his hand and pushed against his chest. He fell back and stared up at Scary as the man looked down at him.

You—he pointed at Scary.

"You want to tell me no?"

He closed his eyes and took a deep breath. The first crush he'd had was on Scary. There was no way in fuck he could've done anything about it. At the age of twelve, it terrified him to admit it to himself. If something's ignored enough, it's like it never existed in the first place. The illusion shattered the moment Scary kissed him. Elijah sat back as if them making out against the office door while Elijah watched was completely normal.

Without opening his eyes, he shook his head. He grunted and started signing—*Does not mean you can boss me around.*

"Of course I can, I always have. Are we getting ready for work or letting Crave play boss tonight?"

Work—He answered and opened his eyes.

"Chicken shit." Scary pressed a hard, quick kiss to his mouth before he pushed himself up.

Scary dropped the towel and grabbed his jeans from the edge of the bed. He watched the flex of bulky muscle beneath inked and hairy skin.

"Keep fucking looking and we ain't working tonight."

He made a go-ahead motion and finished tying his boots. As he stood, Scary's phone started ringing. He reached for it and dragged it off the nightstand.

Scary reached for it and checked the display. His best friend's brow furrowed, and he swiped his thumb across the screen, then he put it on speaker.

"Juvie, you and Elijah having fun?"

Sophie and Elijah were supposed to spend the night there and then come home tomorrow for the weekend. They'd gotten her a phone so she could call any of them or the crew if she needed them.

"Elijah didn't come pick me up."

"Maybe he's just late getting off work."

"Kam said he left at lunch to go to those classes. He texted her that he'd be here to pick me up normal time, but—"

He glanced at Scary. That wasn't like Elijah. If he said he was going to do something especially when it came to Juvie, he didn't go back on his word.

"Is Kam close by?"

He went through the details and what-ifs. There were plenty of positive reasons Elijah was MIA, but his brain went all worst-case scenario.

"Yeah, hold on."

Juvie called Kam, and a few seconds later they heard her voice.

"Hey, Scary, I'm assuming Eli's not there."

"No, we were just getting ready for work. Elijah was supposed to call after him and Juvie got settled in the hotel."

"I called one of the directors of the training program. She said Elijah was there until the end of the class. He got a call as he was leaving. I've called his phone several times, but it goes straight to voice mail."

"Did he check into the hotel?"

"No, he'd made a reservation before our morning meeting."

He waved his hands until he got Scary's attention—
How is our girl?

"How's Juvie?"

"Worried and feeling a bit insecure, but we got her covered. Figure out where Eli is."

"We will," Scary assured her and disconnected the call and instantly made a call. It went straight to Elijah's voice mail.

He didn't know if it would make any difference, but Scary left a message.

"I'm going to call Bull." Scary tapped the screen until ringing filled the room.

He took the phone as Scary turned to sit on the bed. Crave was a damn good bouncer, but he was shit at playing boss. His tendency to throw a punch first and deal with the cops later didn't help the already bad reputation of their bar.

"What," Bull's grumpy voice came over the speaker.

"We need you to babysit tonight."

"No fucking way, man, I'm not—"

"Elijah is MIA. He didn't show to pick Juvie up."

"Ah shit, I got it covered, but if we need to hire new people, I ain't to blame."

"Deal, just don't kill anyone."

"The fuck if I'm gonna guarantee that. You need a backup just call." Bull disconnected the call.

"Let's pack and head out."

They quickly threw a few changes of clothes into a few backpacks. The discussion turned to whether they should call Brody, but decided against it until they had more information. Elijah didn't pull shit like this, but there was one person they needed to contact. He tapped Scary's shoulder.

He made the sign for Peaches, and Scary nodded. They needed a cooler head than they possessed and a lawyer was the one to call.

They made the call and waited while it rang, Scary was about to hang up when Peaches answered.

"Peaches, we need your help."

"Name it."

"Elijah went missing, and we're headed to Atlanta—"

"The cops won't even look at a missing person's report for at least twenty-four hours unless you give them a reason to take it seriously."

He didn't give a fuck about some bullshit minimum time limit. This was Elijah. Their man was responsible, and they knew for sure Elijah would make contact even if it were just five minutes.

"So telling them he didn't show up to pick up his soon-to-be daughter isn't excuse enough."

"He didn't show to pick up Juvie?" Her voice went from calm and rational to concerned.

"No, that's why we called you. We don't fuck with the cops."

"Gib and I will be ready when y'all get here. Pack for a few days?" Peaches asked.

"Yeah."

"We keeping this quiet?"

"For now, he may show up by the time we get to Kam's place. No need to worry anybody until there's a reason."

"Got it. We'll be ready."

Scary slid the phone into his back pocket. He didn't know what they'd do if something happened to Elijah. He started to dip his chin to his chest but stopped when Scary's hands curled around his neck and tugged him forward. Scary nipped gently at his lips.

"Our boy's fine and if he isn't—" Scary growled. "— whoever was stupid enough to fuck with what is ours…pays."

He nodded, and Scary pulled away but not before Scary kissed him long and hard. They parted to pick up their bags and head for the door. The ride ahead of them was going to be long and stressful. Elijah was their redemption, their one bright spot and there wasn't a chance in hell they'd lose him now. He'd already started seeing his life with Elijah and Scary to love and their love in return. A crazy, smart assed kid that he already loved. They were all supposed to have a life. The four of them against the world.

Starting his bike, the deep rumbling growl of the engine didn't soothe him as it had before. They took off toward town to join up with Gib and Peaches. They had to get to Juvie, Elijah would hate for her to be without them—to lose her sense of security.

The cool night air stung his cheeks as he followed behind Scary. He took deep calming breaths as he attempted to focus his chaotic thoughts and tried not to think about Elijah hurt and needing them.

He shook his head. They'd find him, and he'd make damn sure their boy was never out of their sight again. Argument or not, Elijah wouldn't win.

22 THE MOTHERFUCKER BETTER NOT HAVE TOUCHED ELIJAH

Two days and still Elijah's phone went to voice mail. He was about to lose his fucking mind and temper, and Tank not much better. The only person keeping them from falling apart was Juvie. She lay curled up into a tiny ball between them on the bed. Tank occasionally reached out to straighten her blanket or tuck her wavy hair behind her ear.

Lucky had woven one thread wrap into her hair, four tiny bells hung beneath stone beads—the stones were their birthstones. It was Lucky's way of welcoming her to the family. He'd noticed she jingled the bells when she'd get anxious. Of all the fucked up things he'd endured in his life, this turned out to be the only time he felt helpless to make her feel better.

No one heard from Elijah, and they'd reached the point of no return. They needed to notify Brody. Peaches and Gib were taking care of that. They'd retraced Elijah's steps countless times to see if he could find Elijah's car, but nothing. They'd even called every hospital and clinic. The cops were fucking useless.

There was a knock on the door, Scary jumped from the bed as Tank moved in front of Juvie. Kam turned out to be great about them spending time with Juvie when they weren't dealing with reports and their searches. He peeked through the peephole and narrowed his eyes. It was one of Ian's crew. He threw open the door and grabbed the front of the man's shirt. They were about the same height, but the younger man had a good fifty pounds on him.

What worried him the most was the deadness in his black gaze. There was absolutely nothing fucking there.

"Where the fuck is our man," he growled in the stranger's face.

"Got no clue, man."

"Then what the fuck—"

The man cut him off as he tried to shake off Scary's hands. He wasn't letting go until he got answers.

"Few weeks ago, Ian stuck around while we headed out. Something won't right, but won't none of my business. I ain't got much of a conscience. Docs say I'm broken."

"And?" He was losing his fucking patience.

"If there's Karma and all that metaphysical bullshit maybe I gotta make my peace. Did a U-turn 'bout a week back. Went to the motel where Ian was supposed to be hold up. He was acting crazy as fuck." The guy looked passed him, and his eyes widened. "What the fuck you doing with a kid?"

"Our daughter ain't your concern, keep talking."

Massive shoulders shrugged, "I tailed him for a while. Ian started taking an interest in your man, even followed his sweet ass—"

Scary growled and shoved the man into the wall.

"Ya don't take another man's piece. I don't poach on ass I don't own."

The fucker was a god damned sweetheart, but if Ian had Elijah, they had bigger problems than they'd thought.

"Never got close. Just watched him. Fucking weird. Man ain't right."

"I'm losing my fucking patience."

"Whatever, he went to some cabin rental place about an hour passed Powers. He tucked in some supplies. Two days ago, I lost his trail."

"How'd ya find us?"

"Same way I found him, I followed you. After I'd found out where you were staying, I headed back to check out Ian. Didn't see your man though, but I didn't get close. Yesterday he left the cabin. I was gonna nose around a bit, but the managers or whatever got suspicious. I'd hauled ass before the cops showed."

"Why the fuck you so concerned?"

"I ain't, like I said you don't fuck with another man's property."

"Elijah ain't property."

"Man, you're fucking touchy, whatever ya want to call him you don't fuck with it."

Scary stepped back and closed the door. Luckily Juvie hadn't woken up.

"Give me directions to this cabin."

"Got paper?"

He motioned with a nod toward the small table in the corner of the room. A pad with the hotel name and pen sat in the middle of it.

"You got a name."

"Earned the name Psycho after a bar fight, don't much answer to anything else."

"You obviously know us."

"Ian ranted about fags and shit. Not that I didn't see him take a man or two into alleys or motels over the last few years. Figured he was just a hypocrite. He do that to your face?" Psycho aimed the question at Tank.

He noticed Tank stiffen, but he kept tracking Psycho keeping his body between him and Juvie at all times. Psycho didn't seem exactly right in the head. His knuckles were scarred and calloused from years of fighting. The man was a brawler. It took one to recognize one.

If Ian was involved and it wasn't some trap to get Tank back, they needed clear heads. Ian was one vicious motherfucker. He wouldn't hesitate to take Elijah out. Would they even find their man alive? Shit, he couldn't think about that. That wasn't an option for neither him or Tank.

"I ain't here to hurt no one. Ain't my intention to start a fight but I'll sure as fuck finish it." Psycho spoke as he bent and scribbled what he assumed was an address and directions.

"Why are you here then?" He was still leery of the man's motives. It was rare someone did shit without several strings attached. What did he want in exchange for the information?

"Already answered that."

"No, what you said is you don't have a conscience. A man without one wouldn't put his ass on the line for a stranger."

"Just making my peace. Seems like a nice guy y'all got. Not many like us get one that…" Psycho paused. "Pure. Ain't no mistaken that man loves y'all. Gotta be nice."

"You riding with us?" He didn't know what made him ask, but a man like Psycho, crazy or not, he was the type of bastard in your corner.

"Been awhile since I drew some blood, might be fun."

"I thought Crave was bad." He glanced over his shoulder in time to see Tank smile. "We might have found his match."

"Big blond's ain't my type. Ain't he got a thing going with that pretty twink bartender of yours?"

"You notice shit that's for sure."

"Noticing shit keeps ya ass alive."

"Text Kam and when she gets here, we'll head out."

Tank nodded as he retook his place on the bed and started texting Kam with one hand as he comfortingly stroked Juvie's back with the other. It was an action he'd seen Elijah do when putting Juvie to bed.

"Juvie's not gonna be happy," he said as Tank snorted.

Her unhappy was an understatement. She wanted to be there every step of the way. He could see her trying to run into battle right behind them.

"Your daughter's name is Juvie? Is that where you found her?"

"No, it's a nickname, she's a bit too tiny for Crime Boss in training."

"You got a fucking weird ass family, man." Psycho took a seat on one of the uncomfortable looking table chairs.

"Yeah, I do," he said it with a smile as he started packing up his and Tank's things. When he closed in on the bed, he leaned down to give Tank a kiss. It was still odd to be able to do that. "We'll get him back, I promise."

Tank merely nodded his head and turned his attention back to Juvie. He knew Tank was preparing for the worst. Tank knew what Ian could do. And the man was mentally saying goodbye to the little girl they'd begun to consider theirs. If anything happened to Elijah, nothing was holding them back. Killing the fucker would be easy.

"I can't keep one happy, how the fuck you handle two?"

He didn't know why, but he laughed at the question.

"I got fucking lucky I guess."

Two hours later they rode passed the city limit sign. The crew shut down the bar, and they'd sent Twitch home. The Brawler and Twirled Crews prepared to ride to the rescue. He doubted Lucky would let Priest anywhere near violence, but he understood that. Somehow, he knew Priest already experienced enough violence to last him a lifetime.

If they didn't find Elijah breathing and in one piece, Ian wouldn't know what the hell came for him. He knew him and Tank would spend the rest of their lives making sure they made up for their past touching him. He cleared his head and began to plan as he let the wind whip around him and the yellow lines of the road stretch on for miles.

23 COULD THIS MAN BE STUPIDER?

The side of his face swollen and bruised, and Elijah swore he had a molar loose. He tried not to move too much since it sent pain through his ribs. They weren't broken or at least he hoped not. His arms and legs had long since gone numb from being hogtied in an empty room at the back of some cabin. He hadn't exactly made his stay there easier by taunting Ian.

The man was insane. Ian paced the house mumbling to himself. He occasionally heard something shatter. All he could think about were Juvie and his men. He knew he had to make it up to Juvie. He'd promised to pick her up, and he had amazing news for everyone. The placement came through. Juvie would come to live with him.

The distraction of the high he'd received from learning he was going to be a dad caused his carelessness. He hadn't watched where he was going. One second he'd bumped into someone, turned to apologize and next thing he knew, he woke up in the truck of a car. Exhaust and gas fumes twisted his gut, and the stench caused him to throw up. He stunk, he needed to use the bathroom, and his stomach was growling loudly.

He blinked his eyes as they began to burn.

He hadn't spent enough time with Scary and Tank, hadn't decorated Juvie's room, and he was already mourning the life he wouldn't have. All the milestones he'd miss in Juvie's life. The anniversaries and the Sunday rides, nights spent on a barstool at Brawlers as he watched his men work.

Who would've thought straight-laced and always responsible Elijah Vaughn would fall in love with two inked biker bar owners? Much less adopt a smart ass little girl who was more than likely going to follow in her other Daddies footsteps. He closed his eyes as tears trickled from the corners.

It wasn't the time to feel sorry for himself. What would Scary and Tank do? Beat Ian to death and hide the body. Not going to work for him. Skinned knees and bloody noses he could handle, anything above that, and he'd puke. He wouldn't make it as a Brawlers' bouncer, and he'd never hear the end of this.

"What the fuck are you doing here?" Ian's muffled voice came from the outer room.

Elijah could mistake the rage in it.

"Headed back to the west coast. Hiding ain't your strong suit. What the fuck is ya doing playing country boy?"

He didn't recognize the growly voice. None of Ian's crew he'd arrived with spoke, so he couldn't determine which one owned the gravelly voice. Elijah tugged at the ropes, the roughness abraded the skin around his wrists and caused him to hiss. He didn't need two insane men beating the hell out of him at their leisure.

"None of your business."

Ian apparently wasn't excited to see his new visitor.

He struggled to a kneeling position which he found damn near impossible with the way he was tied up, but he finally made it. His fingers ached from the restriction of the rope, and they were clumsy as he tried again to work the knot loose.

He looked up as the door opened and banged against the wall.

"You remember what the fuck happened last time you tried that."

"If you're gonna kill me," he flippantly said.

It was probably best to stop poking the psychopath, but as he said, if Ian ended up killing him what was the point in playing nice.

"Mouthy bitch." Ian brought the back of his hand across his cheek, "All I want—"

The iron tang of blood burst over his tongue. "You tried to kill him."

"No, I didn't. If I wanted him dead, I would've cut his head completely off. The cut was superficial at fucking best."

"Nothing says I love you like a—"

A kick to his already sore ribs took his breath away, and he curled forward as agony went through him. He peeked through his one eye that wasn't almost swollen shut. A man bigger than Scary stood in the doorway. It was the silent man from Brawlers. He wore a bored expression. That look that scared him more than Ian or Elijah's impending death.

"Why are ya fucking around? Just kill him already."

Thanks, asshole, he silently said as he rolled his eyes. Pain shot through his head. Mental note: Don't do that again.

"Shut the fuck up, Psycho, this ain't none of your concern."

Psycho—the man appeared more like a sociopath with the unemotional mask he wore.

"Ya did see his men right? Kill him and get out of town before they come for ya."

"Once this pretty piece of ass if out of the way—"

He snorted. "You think you're going to get Tank back by killing me? Are you off your meds?"

"He needs someone like me, not some suit."

"He's got Scary for that," he said with a smirk but didn't know how well it came across.

Ian's face went red, the veins in his neck and at his temples stood out. He stormed from the room leaving a huge hole in the wall from a single punch.

"You're crazy ya know that, right," Psycho asked, he lazily leaned his bodybuilder sized shoulder against the door frame.

"Actually I'm highly well-adjusted," he quipped. "Wanna help me out here?"

"Not really."

"You're a sweetheart."

"I'm a fucking catch."

It was inappropriate to laugh, but he couldn't help himself.

"I normally like my men tied up and helpless."

"That doesn't sound creepy at all."

Psycho's lips twitched for a microsecond before it completely disappeared.

"Oh, he smiles."

"Have you been like this since he grabbed ya? If so I'm not surprised he's pissed."

"He tried to kill my Tank. I couldn't care less about his feelings."

"But what about your continued breathing?"

"Tank will have Scary, and if they figure out what happened, Ian won't make it to the next sunrise."

"You're vicious for a suit."

"My men are horrible influences."

"I can tell. Juvie's good by the way."

"Did he—If so I'll kill him myself."

"She's fine, last I saw she was asleep with Tank."

He let out a relieved sigh. "She's probably mad at me. I promised to pick her up. We were gonna have dinner, and I was going to surprise her with furniture shopping for her new room." His tears threatened again.

"The Brawlers were about a mile out. They're waiting on confirmation."

"So, what the hell are you waiting for?"

"I want a job."

He suppressed the urge to shake his head as he stared at the apparently crazy man. "Really, you're aiding and abetting a kidnapping for a job interview?"

"Yeah, why not, captive audience and all that."

"Should I ask you if you're off your meds?"

"Don't take that shit, makes me feel outside myself. My rage keeps me alive."

"Are you angry now?"

"Always."

"Wow, if this is rage I wonder if you break a sweat when you're homicidal."

"You want to be saved or what?"

The crazy bastard held up his phone and lifted a thick brow.

"Fine, I've never interviewed hired muscle though."

"Just say I've got the job and we'll move on."

"You've got the job."

As soon as the last word was out of his mouth Psycho lifted the phone to his ear. "Your boy is on site." Without waiting for a response Psycho slid his phone back into his pocket.

"I don't particularly like you."

"No one does, I'm used to it."

Psycho said it so nonchalantly as if the man spoke about the weather. He remembered the guy off sitting by himself with his back to the wall. Did Psycho prefer it that way or was there more hidden behind his coldness? He didn't have long to think about it before Ian pushed passed Psycho's much larger body. Psycho growled at the contact.

The glint of sunlight off steel brought on the first real fear. It wasn't as if he wasn't scared before, but death existed as a concept, but seeing the gun it became real. The cold metal pushed to his temple. The rumble of engines caught their attention.

"How the fuck—"

"That was me," Psycho piped up.

"What the fuck, maybe I should—" Ian swung the gun around as Psycho stepped up until the barrel pressed to the center of his mile-wide chest.

"Go for it, fucker, but make it goddamn count. Cause I'll break your fucking neck before I hit the ground."

He noticed the flinch, a brief moment of fear in the flare of Ian's nostrils and the drain of blood from his face leaving it ashen.

"What ya waiting for, do it." Psycho's voice was cold and lethal.

No doubt Psycho meant it. Ian better kill him, or Psycho would make sure Ian was before Psycho took his final breath.

He felt helpless. Everything he thought of to help out would likely end with Psycho shot. That wouldn't assist anyone in a good way.

"You think I won't," Ian asked with a quavering voice.

"I know you won't. You can bluff your way through the game, but you damn sure ain't got the balls to back it up."

And Psycho said Elijah was crazy. Psycho had a gun to his chest by his own actions and calmly taunted the man.

"Elijah," Scary yelled as he stormed into the room with Tank and the rest of the Brawlers behind him.

He'd never seen a more beautiful sight than his men even with expressions that faltered between concern and rage at equal intervals until anger won out.

"Psycho, back up," Scary ordered.

Elijah started slowly inching his way backward until his toes touched the baseboard.

"Naw, this bastard thinks he's gonna shoot me."

"Kinda noticed that, man."

Tank moved to the right to slide along the wall and eased his way toward him. At least Psycho had Ian distracted. He suddenly realized that was the point. The man put himself on the line—for him. No one except Scary or Tank ever tried to be protective of him before.

"Can't exactly start work if you're dead," he whispered.

There was the microsecond smile again.

"Yes, boss."

"Boss, really?"

"Yeah, you hired me. I've noticed shit, and you're the one in charge. Why ya think I had ya interview me?"

He rolled his eyes. "That was an interview?"

"Shut up," Ian yelled as he tried to re-aim the gun at him.

He froze as he looked into the barrel and lowered his head letting his body fall to the side. A very unmanly yell had him looking up to find Psycho staring down Ian.

Psycho's massive paw clenched around the gun hand, and a scream broke through the tension as he swore he heard bones crack. There was a symphony of groans from the guys crowding the door. Scary moved up to Psycho's side. It was weird to find a man who made Scary look almost slender. He'd never say that aloud though.

"Now, now, fucker, don't mess with the man in charge." Psycho squeezed harder until Ian started to fall to his knees. "I feel all warm and fuzzy toward him."

"Oh, you're so not my type."

"You don't know what you're missing."

His laughter earned him warning rumbles from Scary and Tank.

"Ya know what I said about tied up men."

"What the fuck is going on here," Scary barked the question.

"Nothing," he said as he felt the ropes loosen and he groaned with relief. He was swept up into Tank's arms, and he tried to lift his own to embrace Tank, but they refused to work. Instead of hugging Tank, he buried his face into the curve of Tank's shoulder.

"We'll discuss this later." That statement was a clear warning he and Psycho were in trouble.

He heard a large body hit the floor with a thud and Ian's whimpers.

"We calling the cops," Bull asked.

"I think we can handle this in house. Tank get Elijah out of here. Boys, get moving."

"Don't go to jail, I sure as hell don't have bail enough for the both of you."

Tank stopped beside Scary and Scary grabbed his face in his hands. He gently kissed his swollen eye and bruises.

"I get bailed out first. I can watch that pretty ass better—"

"You don't wanna finish that," Scary warned.

"Can't deny the truth. Shit, I might just poach that ass."

He grabbed Scary's wrists and stared into his eyes. He shook his head, and Scary's eyes narrowed. He'd answer for this later, but he needed to get his thoughts together before he tried to explain. Psycho hid something. Now he was safe and sound with his men he'd figure it out.

Scary kissed him one last time, then Tank carried him through the house. He looked behind Tank to find the Brawlers behind him along with Zerk and Trouble. It finally hit him he was safe as Tank settled him on the front seat of Trouble's truck. Everything he had hurt and the minor things intensified, like being hungry and having to find a bathroom, but he wanted away from that cabin. He just wanted to go home.

"I know you want to go home probably, but you need to see a doctor first. You look like you've gone quite a few rounds with a heavyweight." Trouble's voice was low and concerned from the driver's seat.

"How's Juvie?"

"Her, Kam and Megan are at Twirled House, but you need to get cleaned up first. She's feeling very lost. Scary and Tank tried to make her feel better, but she just keeps asking for you," Zerk answered from over Tank's shoulder.

Tank didn't try to sign, he saw the guilt which quickly replaced the anger of minutes before. "This isn't your fault, he's crazy, and we knew that."

Tank nodded, but he knew he wasn't getting through to the big man.

"I love you." He leaned forward and tenderly pressed his sore lips to the thin, tight line of Tank's mouth.

His heart broke realizing Tank didn't believe it wasn't his fault. After a trip to the hospital and getting Juvie calmed down, he'd take care of Tank. He wasn't going to lose one of his men over this—he refused.

24 SAFE AND SOUND

A month passed and Elijah's cuts and bruises faced, but Tank couldn't let go the fact he'd let Ian hurt Elijah. The man thought he could get him back. He started keeping his distance. Scary and him went a few rounds, but surprisingly Psycho was instigating fights left and right. That fucker truly lived up to his name, yet no one got near Elijah. He didn't like the man's interest at all. What made it worse was that Elijah had a soft spot for the man.

Psycho seemed to garner a perverse amusement from his and Scary's jealousy. They'd watched the man stand with a gun to his chest without a trace of fear. Psycho had a death wish.

He took a Saturday night to himself and planned to hide away in his cabin. In the last few weeks, he spent more time there than at work. He knew it was hurting Elijah, but it also damaged his friendship and new relationship with Scary. Shying away from the affection Scary and Elijah readily tried to give him. The only one he hadn't shut out was Juvie.

She was living with Elijah, enrolled at her new school and settling into her new life. He picked her up as often as he could. Unfortunately, the longer he stayed away from his men, the more insecure Juvie became. He had to try to fix it but couldn't get over the belief what happened to Elijah was his fault.

Psycho and Scary didn't go into many details of what they'd done to Ian. They'd dealt with Ian with all the brutality they possessed. A body hadn't turned up, so Ian was still alive. He regretted that. Ian should have paid more for what he'd done to Elijah. In the days following Elijah's rescue, he'd cataloged every cut and bruise, and committed them to memory.

He had nightmares of what would've happened if Psycho hadn't come to find them—if they hadn't found him in time.

He lifted his fourth beer to his mouth and started to chug the rest of it.

"Done sulking?" Scary's voice came from behind him. "Because I'm fucking tired of kicking your ass."

He flipped Scary off.

"If you're offering." Scary stepped in front of him and jerked him out of the chair.

Scary slammed his mouth down onto his. The kiss was brutal, and he faintly heard the clunk of his bottle hitting the planks of his deck. His body was forced backward into the dim interior of the kitchen. His body heated as a month of holding back and shunning touch slammed into him. Fuck, he'd missed this. He didn't want to be in charge.

Silently he'd broken down, and no one noticed except Elijah and Scary. They sensed when he needed extra anything. Elijah gave him tenderness and compassion, Scary just told him to pull his head out of his ass.

Scary and he hadn't gotten passed kissing, but right then he needed him to—

"I'm not going to punish you. Yes, I know what you're thinking. It's not happening," Scary stopped them beside the bed. "Elijah would be pissed at me. Lift your arms, baby."

He quickly obeyed, and Scary pushed his hands beneath Tank's t-shirt. Scary quickly removed the cotton. Then Scary jerked his belt undone. It made a soft sound as the leather slid through the belt loops. Scary made quick work of shoving the denim down until Tank could kick them aside.

He plucked at the fabric covering Scary's stomach.

"Nope, this is my show." Scary wrapped his hand around Tank's dick. "And this is fucking mine."

His eyes widened as Scary dropped to his knees. Scary quickly swallowed him to the root. His fat cock pushed at the back of Scary's throat. He dropped his head back onto his shoulders at the pleasure that made his thighs shake, and he had to lock his knees.

Scary's fingertips brutally sunk into the backs his legs. Scary bobbed along his shaft sucking with almost painful pressure until Tank couldn't resist moving. He fucked Scary's mouth, the man's long goatee tickled his aching balls. The calloused palms and fingertips of Scary's hands stroked up the back of his thighs to grip his ass. Scary dug into his crease, his middle fingers massaging Tank's hole. He clenched at the ecstasy. No one had fucked his ass in years. He hadn't trusted them, not like he did Scary or Elijah.

He wanted the stretch and burn, wanted to feel Scary the next fucking day. It should feel weird, but it was just right. He curved his hands around Scary's stubbly head loving the rasp of it under his palms. He lifted his head and caught sight of Elijah leaned back against the wall beside the door.

Scary released his cock with a wet pop.

"On the bed, hands and knees."

He almost hesitated, momentarily worried about how Elijah felt. Elijah's heavy-lidded eyes and the visible bulge of his hard dick eased his apprehension. He noticed Elijah started removing his clothes as Tank turned to crawl onto the bed. Tank glanced over his shoulder and found Scary and Elijah naked, kissing roughly. Their hands moved over each other in desperation.

His cock jerked between his thighs at the picture they made. They broke the kiss, and Scary moved to the foot of the bed while Elijah strode to the nightstand. Scary's huge hands squeezed his ass and pulled the cheeks apart, then Scary's warm breath fanned over his hole. He grunted as Scary pressed his tongue against the wrinkled skin, sucking and stabbing until he pushed inside. Tank groaned as he dropped his forehead to the covers and clenched them in his fists.

Scary fucked him, pressing his face deep between his cheeks. Tank rolled his hips trying to get closer. Elijah's slender fingers combed through Tank's hair, and Tank lifted his head. Elijah's soft lips conformed to his.

"Elijah wants to watch me fuck your tight ass," Scary rumbled against his back as he kissed up the indent of his spine. "See his men get off for him. Do you want that," Scary asked as he pulled at Tank's left cheek and Scary's dick rubbed over his hole.

Even if Tank could speak, he wouldn't have been able to as Scary's shaft rode the cleft of his ass. He opened his mouth to moan and Elijah's tongue speared inside. Scary sucked at the back of his neck as the hair on Scary's chest scraped his back. It was like sensory overload, he couldn't focus on either.

His body shook as the broad head of Scary's cock nudged at his opening. He shoved his hips backward as he felt the burn as Scary stretched him. Tank grabbed Elijah's hands as Scary popped inside.

"Fuck, don't—" Scary froze behind him.

He knew there was nothing between them. Scary was sliding into him raw and bare. Tank broke the kiss as he clenched his teeth. He grunted in protest when Scary pulled out pushing back to get Scary back inside. His patience was growing thin. Tank wanted to be fucked hard and rough—wanted to feel Scary filling him with cum.

"Condom," Scary's voice tight as he asked.

Elijah shifted on the bed and Tank realized Elijah was handing Scary a condom and lube.

"I'll take your tight ass bare soon, but not tonight."

Tank nodded his head, reached back to wrap his hand around Scary's right thigh as the cool lube trickled over his hole.

"Elijah on your back, Tank, suck our boy's cock while I fuck this pretty hole." Scary's thumb spread the slick and pushed inside, shallowly fucking Tank's ass.

Tank rode the thick digit as he watched Elijah lie down on his back. Elijah wrapped his hand around his slender cock with flushed tip. Tank swallowed the hole length and choked as Scary shoved inside with one powerful thrust. He hadn't even realized Scary had replaced his thumb with his cock.

Sweaty skin slapped together as Scary's hips slammed against his ass. Tank desperately sucked Elijah's cock as Elijah moaned and shook beneath him. Tank looked up from under his lashes to find Elijah watching Scary fucking Tank. Elijah plucked at his beaded nipples, his pinked skin covered in a sheen of sweat. Their man planted his feet on the mattress fucking into Tank's mouth. Elijah's thick, pubic curls tickled his nose as his throat convulsed around the head.

Elijah's whimpers joined Scary and Tank's grunts as Scary plowed Tank in brutal jabs. The barbells along the underside of Scary's cock torturing his prostate. Elijah tapped his shoulder and Tank released his cock. Elijah scooted beneath him. A condom was quickly smoothed down his cock and Elijah positioned Tank to his hole.

"You two—s'good, sexy," Elijah could barely speak with his labored breaths. "Fuck me," Elijah ordered.

Scary's next thrust forced him passed the slight resistance of Elijah's body. Tank threw his head back as he yelled. The bulk of Scary's body pushed him down on top of Elijah. Scary's momentum causing Tank's cock to fuck Elijah's ass. Tank suspended between the burning pleasure of Scary's possession and the tight, clench of Elijah squeezing him in a vice.

Tank tried to keep his weight off Elijah by bracing his elbows on either side of his head. His balls drew up tight, his muscles clenched and he hung suspended between his men. Scary's growls vibrated against his throat. Elijah rolled his hips rubbing his cock between their bellies.

"Come on my cock. Show me how much you fucking…" Scary's piston hard snaps of his hips sped up, "Love me inside you. You've always wanted my cock, tell me yes," Scary ordered.

Tank quickly nodded his head. His hair stuck to his sweaty face.

"Dreamed of this?"

Tank nodded again. He had before he'd pushed aside the stupid wants and after Scary kissed him. Tank clenched his fists in Elijah's hair as he held his mouth to Elijah's as Elijah tried to hold both him and Scary. Elijah screamed as the smaller man came between them. Heat spread between their bodies. At the brutal clenching of Elijah's body, he couldn't hold off, he groaned long and loud as his dick pulsed in agonizing pleasure.

"Both so fucking sexy, mine, both...of...you." Scary's thrusts faltered as he pushed once more until he caused Tank's body to bow and sink deeper into Elijah. The trembling body beneath him and the shaking one on top too much and his cock jerked in time with Scary and Elijah's until they collapsed exhausted to their sides causing him and Scary to slip free. All three of them groaned at the loss.

The kisses were lazy and slow, hands stroked tenderly as he weakly signed I love you to both of them. He closed his eyes as he tried to control himself. So many years he'd waited for someone, since he had it times two, he didn't know how to handle it. It was too much.

♦ ♦ ♦

It was after midnight, and they curled up on either side of Elijah. They hadn't spoken afterward. Each seemed lost in their own thoughts. Elijah rubbed his and Scary's hips. He was the first to break the silence.

"I love you both, but, Tank, if you pull this again, I won't be responsible for what I do. None of what happened with Ian is your fault. The man was insane."

Tank signed *I'm sorry.*

"No, nothing to be sorry for. This is everything I want. You and Scary, raising Juvie and being a family. I won't settle for anything less."

"Elijah's right. This is our chance—our redemption. Let us have one good fucking thing. Us with Elijah, raising our daughter as weird as that sounds."

Elijah smacked Scary's hip as Scary chuckled.

"Now where are we going to live," Elijah asked.

"This is a little far out for Juvie to catch the bus. Your place is okay, Elijah, but I've got the rooms. You need an office, we have our room, and then there's an extra room for Juvie."

"We can keep it for getaways when we need alone time."

Tank liked the sound of that and nodded. He'd built this place secretly thinking one day he'd have someone of his own. Now he had two and a daughter, and Juvie liked it out there. Scary's was even closer to Brawlers.

"So, we're in agreement," Elijah asked.

Scary and he nodded. Elijah turned on his side with his back to Tank as Scary scooted closer to wrap his arm around them. He closed his eyes at the contentment he felt. Tank kept them away for too long. As great as the sex was, this was the part he loved. The freedom to touch and hold his two men. He wouldn't take it for granted again. As Scary said, it was their redemption. They finally had the family they'd always wanted. He glanced at Scary, and the man leaned forward to brush their mouths together. Scary pulled back, and Tank signed *I love you.*

"Don't you fucking forget it."

Tank smiled as he let his eyes close and couldn't wait to begin his life without the specters of the past suffocating him.

EPILOGUE: ADOPTION DAY

A month later...

It was finally official, Scary leaned back on one the loungers in the backyard that was filled with both Twirled and Brawlers Crews. Throw in the Trenton's and it was a freak fest for their daughter's first official afternoon as a member of the family. He didn't think Juvie believed it until that day when the judge signed the adoption papers.

They'd all held their breaths. A so-called single man and gay as well they'd tried to be optimistic, but pessimism bled into their minds. Juvie hadn't moved from one of their sides all afternoon as if she didn't believe it yet.

At the moment, she was on Tank's lap who she'd started calling Dad, while Elijah was Daddy, he'd earned the name Papa. Lucky broke into his house a few days ago to redo Juvie's room. It looked like the Twirled House threw up in Juvie's bedroom. They'd move in over the weekend. Elijah packed two weeks ago and had slowly brought things over. Monday Elijah's house would go on the market.

Juvie also had a whole new wardrobe courtesy of Lucky and his sewing machine which she'd find tonight along with the surprise of her room. Her hair even acquired a few new wraps, and her ears earned another piercing. Zerk even broke out the airbrush to tattoo her a few full sleeves. He was worried she'd get overwhelmed with all the attention, but she seemed to love it.

"I want one, Priest, come on," Lucky whined and stomped behind Priest.

"I can't breed, we've talked about this. I'm not arguing about this. I said no when you tried this shit after Trouble got with Brody." Priest picked up his pace trying to put more distance between him and Lucky.

"I'll bribe Lou for womb space, please!" Lucky's please drew out for at least a full minute. "I want a ginger."

He heard Elijah laughing behind him and then he had a lap full of his man. "Are those two ever going to admit they're dating?"

"Fuck if I know, Lucky's been sniffing around that ass since Priest showed up."

"I've heard the stories. Priest barely uses his room because he's sleeping in Lucky's almost every night."

"They'll figure it out or continue to be best friends. How's our Juvie?"

"I think she's okay, but she's good at putting on a brave face."

"We're good, all of us. She's got the papers, and it's all fucking official."

"I know, but we've been sweating this for a month wondering. She didn't want to get too comfortable if this was like her previous homes."

"Well it's not, she's ours. Ain't no doubt about that now."

Scary looked over at Tank to find the man smiling at him and Elijah. He tipped his chin to signal Tank to bring Juvie over. Scary curled up to kiss Elijah quickly. Tank knelt beside the lounger and Juvie stayed standing with her forearm resting on Tank's shoulder.

"Elijah, we wanted…" Scary cleared his throat. Fuck this was harder than he thought. "Listen we know it can't be all official and shit, but we wanted to know if you wanted to make honest men out of us?"

Elijah's mouth fell open, and Juvie giggled.

Tank held up his hand and dumped three rings from a small velvet bag onto his palm.

"We definitely ain't prizes, but—"

Elijah's mouth slammed onto his and then disappeared as Elijah threw himself at Tank.

"Hey, you're gonna lose them, Daddy," Juvie dropped to her knees and picked up the rings that fell to the ground.

"Are y'all fucking kidding me?"

"Hey, little ears, she's already foul-mouthed enough." Scary chuckled as Juvie sucked her teeth and rolled her eyes.

She held out her tiny hand with the rings filling her palm.

"No, we love you, every crazy inch of you, not so much your new bodyguard." He nodded toward Psycho who watched Elijah and Juvie like a hawk. The man took his job seriously inside and outside Brawlers.

"Psycho is a sweetheart in a weird way. I love y'all too, but marriage? Y'all never mentioned it before."

"Like I said it won't be official, just a commitment ceremony so that all three of us can say all those beautiful vows. We wanted to make today special. Our family being all legal."

Tank signed asking did Elijah want to and Scary could tell he was as nervous as him.

Marriage was an enormous fucking step for all of them. They'd worked their ass off to make their relationship work and get that far. All they wanted was to have their man stand in front of their friends and family as they committed to each other forever. Because this was it for them.

"Tank, Elijah, wanna be official with me?"

Tank and Elijah leaned in and hugged him, they both nodded. They slipped on the rings as everyone whooped and passed out shots around them. All three of them reached out an arm and pulled a smiling Juvie between them.

They didn't have to do it tomorrow, next month or even next year, he knew the rings were enough for them. But he wanted to ask them, to show his men he loved them. This is what he and Tank escaped their old lives for, a chance at redemption and a different life—something better and that's what they got.

THE END

ABOUT THE AUTHOR

By day, J.M. is an introverted cook hiding out in her kitchen in the middle of nowhere Ohio, by night and any free time she may have, she is a writer of mainly LGBTQ Fiction and Erotica. Although. she's equal opportunity when it comes to telling a story, she'll even write a bit of straight erotic romance when the mood strikes.

She has been writing for years in old notebooks. At the age of eight, she wrote the worst poem in the history of poetry, but it sparked her love for writing. She reads too much and loves to get lost in other worlds and her favorite stories have to include laughter and having the reader doing at least one double take. Thirty-something, forever restless she uses her stories to ground herself, and find her place of peace.

WHERE TO FIND J.M.
www.jmdabneyauthor.com

AVAILABLE NOW

LUCKY
Twirled World Ink 4

Welcome to Twirled World Ink where the crazies run the asylum.

When someone is asked to describe crazy, if they know Lee "Lucky" Trenton, they'd point at him. Accident prone and without a filter of any kind to tell him to shut up before he says something inappropriate, he's no one's idea of a perfect partner. Growing up with parents who subscribed to a philosophy of Radical Honesty, Lucky and his siblings were doomed from the womb. Lucky found a home away from home at Twirled World Ink, but he didn't just find a place to belong...he'd found Priest.

Matthew "Priest" Beall ran away from his judgmental family the second he'd earned enough money. He'd come in search of Gib Phelps a legend in the tattoo industry. If you wanted to learn the craft, then he was the man to beg for an apprenticeship with, and he'd begged. Priest might have left the violence of his past behind, but when he closed his eyes, it comes back to torture him. The only place he felt safe was when his best friend Lucky let him sleep in his arms. He wanted more, but he didn't think he deserved it.

Priest left his family behind without regret only to find a new one with the crew of Twirled World and the super weird Trenton family. Could he grab onto his new life or would the memories of the past ruin the happiness he'd gained?

✦ ✦ ✦

1 ENTER THE HYPER HIPPE

Lee "Lucky" Trenton adjusted his ear buds and lifted his sketchpad from atop a stack of tattoo mags. He winced as his slowly healing sprained wrist reminded him of his latest accident. Since he'd first started walking, he fell at least once a week. It didn't help that his long gangly frame and oversized feet made him a moving hazard. He looked like a fucking scarecrow and about as attractive as one too.

He had no misconceptions about the power of his looks. Odd in temperament, personality and shape, it was what it was. He'd hit his peak at sixteen reaching a super leanly muscled six-three and there his growing ceased. It wasn't so bad. At twenty-eight he worked with a world-renowned group of tattoo artists. He'd worked his ass off from apprentice to well-respected member of Twirled World Ink. So, he didn't have many complaints about where his life was going, well except one—Matt "Priest" Beall.

The sexy fucker was his co-worker of five years and had driven him to the point of sexual frustration induced insanity since Gib introduced the short, husky bear as the newest artist. When Priest entered the zone, no one rivaled his confidence and talent but introduce flirting, and the man went terminally shy. Priest also had the cutest fucking stutter he'd ever heard.

Not that Priest noticed him. Priest relegated him to best friend status along with the rest of the Twirled World Crazies. Priest was completely oblivious to his interest or clues. Lucky's frustration levels hit the point of pulling a fucking caveman, bashing Priest over the head and dragging him to his lair. Sadly, that probably wouldn't work either. Landon Phelps, the big boss' son, tried to offer him advice, but again the more he tried to make his intentions known the more clueless Priest became. So, in the end, he'd sworn Landon to secrecy and decided being around Priest was enough.

Although watching all those hot guys try to get at his man threatened to turn him homicidal. All types tried to make a play for Priest, big heavily tattooed Bears or pretty and perfect barely legal boys and every type in between. The only saving grace really was Priest didn't jump at the not so subtle invites. Although those blushes that stained Priest's tanned cheeks above his beard were like waving a red flag at a rampaging bull—it was all challenge. Lucky wasn't intimidating enough to scare them away or even make his claim on Priest appear serious.

Scary, the shop manager, with one terrifying glance got the men to start running, but Scary wasn't around all the time.

Scary owned a bar named Brawlers. The name was self-explanatory. The cops hated the place, but the bodies and blood were normally nowhere in sight, and no one would talk by the time they showed up.

He cursed as his mind wandered and brought his attention back to Priest who was handling the phones and desk, scheduling appointments and consultations. Aside from Trouble, who was exactly how he sounded, Priest was the best one to deal with the public. He tended to talk to himself and what came out wasn't always flattering, so Lucky was banned from all business except ink. Which suited him fine, he was ecstatic to spend his time drawing until they assigned him a client or one requested him.

His phone started repeating The Wicked Witch is Calling in a terrified shriek, and he grabbed his phone. He tugged his earbuds out as he stroked his thumb across the screen and answered. "Hello, Ma."

"How is my least fucked up child doing today?"

A picture of the five-foot-nothing hellion known as his mother flashed in his head. For all the innocuous appearance of Lily, she was the poster child for heavy medication. He loved the crazy bitch.

"Your least fucked up child hasn't broken a bone and the day is almost over." His friends snickered from across the room, and he flipped them off without even glancing at them.

He'd grown up in a household that subscribed to a rule of radical honesty. No lies and the only rule was don't have the cops come to the house. Which in hindsight he had to admit his parents were fucking geniuses—no rules equaled no rebellion.

"What about stitches?"

"I assure you I'm free of new scars." He probably jinxed himself.

"How's the sex life?"

From any other mother the question would sound weird and creepy, but in his house growing up conversations about sex were open and non-judgmental. He hadn't even come out. The day his family found out he was gay was when he brought his first boyfriend home when he was thirteen.

"I'm a fucking monk," he muttered with deep disgust.

"Pathetic, young one, truly pathetic. Even your personality-less brother is getting some."

"He only gets ass because he pays well for it." The old joke made his mother cackle. Linus was socially awkward but always had a new woman on his arm every time he came home.

"It's still getting laid."

"I know, I'm an utter disappointment."

"Yes, you are."

"Thanks, Ma, I love you too."

"I've allowed you to survive for twenty-eight years, I assure you that took a lot of moral fortitude."

His impending death was an old threat. Out of Linus and Lucky's twin sister, Leigh-Lou, he was the most like his parents.

"I am appreciative that you granted me my continued breathing. Now, what do you want?"

"We're having an intervention. Your father and I think it's time you lose that pesky virginity."

"Ma, I haven't been a virgin since I was fifteen. As well you know since you bought me the condoms because you said me breeding would lessen the IQ of the next generation of Trenton progeny. Although, being gay and breeding—"

"You haven't decided to spread the seed through IVF because I'm sorry to say my hopes are your sister will carry on the line."

The horror in her voice at the thought he'd want to bring a child into the world made him lose it. He ignored the eye rolls and strange looks he noticed when he spun his chair to catch sight of his best friends. They stared at him with something close to horror in their gazes. His family's antics were well known. Although he was careful to make sure none of his friends, especially Priest, were left alone with any of his family they were aware of the damaged genes he carried.

"Yes, Leigh-Lou would be best to have the next gen, I mean really her *men are good for only one thing philosophy* is bound to catch up with her." His highly sexual twin didn't believe in monogamy or relationships, as soon as a man mentioned the c-word she was gone before the third syllable was out of their mouths.

"Leave your twin alone, at least she isn't sniffing some dude's ass and doesn't have the balls to pounce on it."

"And people wonder why I'm weird."

"You're the normal one, that's why we stopped asking you to attend functions for my side of the family. We can only take so much embarrassment."

"Just call me the dark family secret. So, we've discussed the ban on me discussing future children with my non-existent partner. How much I'm an embarrassment. The disappointment in my sex life that is no better than a eunuch's, so what the hell did you want?"

"My mother-in-law is coming for her annual inspection, and as per her request, all the fruits of her son's loins must be in attendance so she may count piercings, tattoos and whether the fuck of the year matches the one from last year.

"I swear that woman lives to ruin my fun. Your father has already hidden my scarf skirts and tasseled pasties. The man has been living in sin with me for nearly thirty-five long years. It's like the fucker doesn't know me yet."

"Hid the tasseled pasties, he must die! What about the sequined middle finger ones I made you for Mother's Day when I was ten? I made them extra-large since you said we ruined your nipples. Those would fit the occasion." The gagging behind him made him snort. That's what they get for being nosy.

"Those too. Like I said, he's putting a crimp in my fucking style. He knew I was weird the night we met. He fooled me. If I knew about his boring family, I would've kept my panties on."

"Well, how could you resist his line about the dashboard lights bringing out the green in your eyes? Or how *Grateful Dead* just built the sexual tension to combustible levels?"

"So, you be there at one and don't be late. Wear a sleeveless shirt, holey jeans and make sure your dreads are extra high on your head. Do you have that six-gauge septum bone horn? Do you have a date? Maybe one you can bring on a leash? I can only take an hour of that woman before I gotta bring out the hookah."

"Should I pull a big brother and pick up a trick from the street corner?"

"Oh, you do love me," she squealed. "Make sure they look like a case of antibiotics waiting to happen. I'll make sure I get a case of antibacterial sanitizer and spray."

"Okay, I'll see you Sunday."

"I'm rather fond of you at the moment."

"I'm fond of you too, Ma." The call disconnected and the silence in the shop made him turn to catch the stares.

"What the fuck is wrong with your family," Scary demanded.

"Nothing, why?"

"I think I threw up in my mouth a bit," Trouble gagged and reached for the trash can.

"Dude, you've met my family. You love my mother."

"Not enough to know about her ruined nipples," Trouble screeched.

"A year of breastfeeding—" He ducked the arsenal of pens Trouble aimed at his head.

"Did your mother do high quantities of drugs when she was pregnant?" Zerk shook his head.

"I think she did a bunch of acid before the rabbit died."

"That would explain it."

"Fuck you, guys, my mother is a fucking saint."

"No, she's heavily medicated, but I think that started long before the kids." Zerk gathered up his stuff and backpack. "I'm going to the back. I'm destined to have nightmares tonight."

The big gruff man took off at a run. Scary wasn't far behind, but he wasn't running—just disgusted.

People would think something was wrong with his family. They were as normal as the next just with a few extra quirks.

"It wasn't that fucking bad," he yelled at Zerk's retreating form. "You ain't got something to say," he asked Priest.

"I like your mother."

"That's because I've never left you alone with her. You're coming to dinner this Sunday."

"Oh—no, no I can't do that. Your sister grabbed my—" Priest lowered his voice. "—junk last time. She's been texting me for months. I still don't know how she got my number."

"She swiped it from my phone. Doesn't matter you're coming. I'll give you mace. It won't put the she-devil down for long, but it'll give you enough time to make a run for it and scream for help."

"Maybe a taser or better yet a cattle prod, that way he won't have to get close to her. She gets within a few feet, he can shock her." Trouble set the trashcan back down and sent Priest a sympathetic look.

"That's my sister, man."

"Yeah, I know, but it's true. I screamed at her I was gay the first time I met her because the sex-starved expression made me feel dirty. I thought I was gonna need a shower."

"Yeah, the shrieked panic coming out when five-foot of nothing wasn't even near you wasn't unmanly at all. If I remember, you shoved your innocent boyfriend in front of you like a shield."

"Brody is bi, he's seen pussy before."

"Her pussy wasn't out. Her skirt wasn't that short."

"Dude, we could almost see if she waxed—" Trouble gagged.

"I'm going to get coffee."

"Pick me up—"

"No, you're on your own. Get your pretty husband to get you your coffee. Priest, you want something," he asked the silent man.

"Thanks, my usual. Do I really have to go with you Sunday?"

"Yes," Lucky answered and left the shop. Then what he'd done hit him. Priest attended plenty of Lucky's family dinners, but not when the Grand Monster made her yearly inspection. He was going to subject Priest to full-on family crazy dysfunction. The only thing he could hope was his family kept his secret, but secrets and lies never remained hidden. He was fucked and not in the way he wanted to be, fucking great. Bribes, he needed lots and lots of bribes or spiked drinks. If they were sleeping, they couldn't talk. The thought buoyed his spirits, and he smiled to himself with a plan forming.